THE UND...

CHASING PRINCES

FROM USA TODAY BESTSELLING AUTHOR
ERIN BEDFORD

Chasing Princes © 2019 Embrace the Fantasy Publishing, LLC

All rights reserved under the International and Pan-American Copyright Conventions. No part of this book may be reproduced or transmitted in any form or by any means, electronic or mechanical, including photocopying, recording, or by any information storage and retrieval system, without permission in writing from the publisher.

This is a work of fiction. Names, places, characters and incidents are either the product of the author's imagination or are used fictitiously, and any resemblance to any actual persons, living or dead, organizations, events or locales is entirely coincidental.

Warning: the unauthorized reproduction or distribution of this copyrighted work is illegal. Criminal copyright infringement, including infringement without monetary gain, is investigated by the FBI and is punishable by up to 5 years in prison and a fine of $250,000.

Also by Erin Bedford

The Underground Series
Chasing Rabbits
Chasing Cats
Chasing Princes
Chasing Shadows
Chasing Hearts
The Crimes of Alice

The Mary Wiles Chronicles
Marked by Hell
Bound by Hell
Deceived by Hell
Tempted by Hell

Starcrossed Dragons
Riding Lightning
Grinding Frost
Swallowing Fire
Pounding Earth

The Celestial War Chronicles
Song of Blood and Fire

The Crimson Fold
Until Midnight
Until Dawn
Until Sunset
Until Twilight

Curse of the Fairy Tales
Rapunzel Untamed
Rapunzel Unveiled

Her Angels
Heaven's Embrace
Heaven's A Beach

Heaven's Most Wanted

House of Durand
Indebted to the Vampires
Wanted by the Vampires

Academy of Witches
Witching On A Star
As You Witch
Witch You Were Here
Just Witch It

Granting Her Wish
Vampire CEO

THE UNDERGROUND BOOK THREE

CHASING PRINCES

FROM USA Today BESTSELLING AUTHOR
ERIN BEDFORD

CHAPTER 1

CONSEQUENCES

MY PALMS WERE sweating and my heart raced as my eyes trained on the kitchen table where my cell phone sat, waiting for me to have the guts to pick it up. Sitting in one of my grandmother's mismatched chairs, I chided myself for being such a wuss.

Get it together, Kat. What would Alice think if she saw you now?

Alice, for a lack of a better word, was sloppy. For someone who grew up in a time where it was all about refinement and propriety, once the human turned Fae was allowed to let her hair down, she went all out.

Clothing was strewn everywhere, dishes left in the sink, and the potato chips. I have never seen anyone eat as many chips as that woman did. For all her faults, it didn't keep her from losing the snotty attitude she came with.

Fortunately, she was not there to see what a wet fish, as she would say, I was being. It was just a silly phone call, one that I dreaded, but was necessary for the survival of not just Alice, but me as well.

Snatching the phone up before I could talk myself out of it again, I punched the speed dial for my parent's house.

"Please don't let Mom pick up. Please," I muttered to myself as the phone rang in my ear. I waited. After the sixth ring, I was sure they weren't going to pick up, and I would be forced to wait until later to get the courage to do it all over again, but on the seventh ring, a familiar stern voice answered.

"Nottington Residence."

"Hillary!" I could almost cry at the sound of her permanently grumpy voice. "How are you?"

"I am well, Katherine. What do you want?" Her voice had a sharp, no nonsense sting to it. I'd have been offended if it wasn't just the way Hillary was.

"Actually, I was calling to talk to my dad. Is he around?" I chewed on the nail of my thumb as I waited for her to answer.

"Yes, I will get him. Hold —" A voice in the background cut her off and then she said the words I dreaded to hear, "Here's your mother."

My heart tightened in my chest and a stutter-filled my voice, "No. Wait. I'll call back-" I tried to get out before she handed the phone over, but I was too late.

"Katherine, so nice of you to call after all this time."

"Hello, Mom," I grumbled. "And it hasn't been that long."

"Two weeks is a long time to an old woman like myself." She sniffed over the phone. "Your father and I were starting to worry you would never call. Though, I have no idea why you are the one who so rudely darted out on dinner like the devil himself was on your heels."

Gritting my teeth, I clutched the edge of the table in front of me. The night she was talking about was not a fond one. It was the night that Chess had met my family, and like all my family gatherings, it ended with me feeling like complete and utter trash. It was my mother's fault as usual but trying to explain that to her was a wasted effort that I didn't really have time for.

"I'm sorry I ruined dinner, but that isn't what I called for."

"Well then, what did you call for?" My mother hummed at me. "It better not be to help you find another job after you got yourself fired from the last one. I've used up most of my favors in this town for you already."

The reminder of my recent unemployment stung and only served to remind me why the call was so important.

"No, Mom. I don't need another job."

"Then you found one already?" her voice was filled with sarcastic glee. I didn't know why she bothered asking when she knew I had done no such thing. Word traveled fast in our town, and if I had a new job, she would have known before I did.

"No, not yet." I crossed one leg over the other, kicking the bottom of the table in an effort to relieve some of my anxiety.

My mother gave an impatient sigh, and I could practically see her roll her eyes at me through the phone. "Well, Katherine, I don't know how you are going to survive without a job. There is still money in the account we opened under your name from when you were younger. Not that you ever used it." She snorted. "It's not a bad thing to have money, dear. You shouldn't feel bad about relying on your parents that's what we are here for."

I was actually shocked she had even brought up giving me money. That was the exact reason I had called, and the fact that she was offering it up to me without having to pull teeth made me suspicious.

"That would be helpful." My words were cautious and questioning. "But what do you want in return?"

"Return?" My mother's voice hit a higher pitch, and I definitely knew she wanted something. "Why can't a mother just give her daughter the support she needs without wanting anything in exchange?"

"Because, this is you we're talking about, Mom. Not Mother Teresa." The back door opened and I looked up from the table to see Alice float in.

Gone were the yoga pants, in their place were a pair of black dress pants and a light blue blouse, which really brought out the color of her eyes. It had taken some work, but I had finally gotten her away from the daytime television, and out into the human world.

I pointed at the phone and mouthed, "Mom." Alice nodded her head in understanding before moving to the refrigerator. Grabbing a bottle of water, she sat down at the table opposite me and waited.

"Well," my mother continued, "Now that you mention it, Margery down at the city council is looking for an assistant for her new group she is forming against this outbreak of creatures." The way she said the word creatures didn't hide her disdain in the slightest.

It started with the faeries and then my mother using that sweet troll, Bar. But not long after that, Fae began pouring out of the Underground like it was on fire. I hadn't been back since my confrontation with my mother in her throne room, it very well could be.

It was quickly discovered that the portal in the woods behind my house was not the only portal to our world. The door in the Between could lead to anywhere in the world, and the Fae took that opportunity to make their presence known. And at the center of the outpour was our little town.

When I asked Alice why they would want to come here of all places when they could go anywhere in the world, she had just looked at me like I was stupid.

"Wouldn't you want to be near the one with the most power?" She'd asked as if it was clear as day who she was talking about.

The Fae kept reminding me that I was the savior, the one that would be the end of the shadows and ruler of their world. I wasn't even sure I could rule myself, let alone a whole kingdom.

"Those creatures are called Fae, Mom. They've already said so on the news, you could at least give them their proper name if you are going to be prejudice." I shared a look with Alice who rolled her eyes.

"Prejudice! Katherine Marie, don't you dare call me prejudice. I have no problem with any *human* of another race, religion, or sexual orientation. But these aren't humans. They're monsters!" Her voice rose to the screeching pitch that made my ears ring. "Have you even seen some of these so-called Fae? They're little more than animals. Just this morning there was one on the Ellen show with huge feet and bulbous eyes. And those fangs! Hillary had to turn off the television before I fainted." She paused in her rant. "They are not people, Katherine. They are monsters, and they must be eradicated." My mother let out a deep breath and seemed to compose herself. "So, I will let Margery know you will be down tomorrow to help her with the rally."

"That's not going to happen," I snapped.

"I don't see why you are so set on accepting these things. What does Chess think of all this? He seemed like such a nice man, certainly, he sees the right way of things."

"I wouldn't know. I haven't seen him." At the mention of Chess, something sharp pinched in my chest.

It was true; I hadn't seen Chess, not since he was taken by the Seelie Queen. I had no doubt her taking him was a power play, a way to punish me for my actions in her court.

"What do you mean you haven't seen him? Don't tell me you two broke up already?" My mother scoffed. "You really need to learn to hold on to a man or you'll never be as happy as your sister is with Simon."

"We weren't dating to begin with, so it doesn't matter." I shrugged, my eyes began to burn, and I turned from Alice so she wouldn't see my distress.

Chess' capture notwithstanding, we hadn't been on the best of terms when he was taken. When a girl tells a guy she loves him, she expects at least some kind of response. An 'I love you too' or a 'Go to hell', but Chess wasn't like other men. He was a Fae, and a womanizing Fae at that. I should have expected the nonchalant response he had given me.

Wasn't it me who kept claiming we were just friends? Why should sleeping together make that any different? My declaration had done nothing but solidify my reasoning as to why I needed to stay away from men altogether. So far they had done nothing but make my life more complicated. My first love as a Fae was a prime example of my failure in the relationship department.

"Well, you should call him up and try to work it out. Your father and I really liked him, and he seemed to adore you. Men like that are hard to find."

My mother's praise of Chess made me laugh. She, who was just ranting about the creatures, was half in love with one herself. I was half tempted to burst her little bubble and let her know exactly what kind of man Cheshire S. Cat was.

Alice placed her hand on mine, and I glanced up at her with a small smile. "I'll take it under advisement. I really need to go now, Mom. Will you have a new card issued to me for the account?" I held my breath as I waited for her to respond.

I had no inclination to join their hate rally, especially since I was mostly Fae myself. How would it look, the Seelie Princess supporting the extermination of her own kind? The thought of it was so ironic I almost wanted to go to the event just to see what would happen.

"Yes, yes of course. I can't have my daughter starving, now can I? But you'll think about the rally? I mean, you don't have to participate but a show of support would make a world of difference."

"I can't make any promises, but I'll think about it. Bye, Mom." I clicked the phone off and dropped my head to the table with a thud. Wincing at the dull pain in my head, I looked to Alice. "So, how did it go?"

"Not very well, I am sorry to say." Alice laced her fingers together on the table as prim as could be. Even dressed like a modern woman, she still couldn't get past her late 1800s upbringing.

I grunted and glared down at the table. Things were not looking good for us.

While exploring the modern human world, Alice had come across several other Fae who, like her, were stuck in this realm with no other choice but to try to make the best of it. In a few short days, she had formed a coalition of Underground creatures. This collective was mostly made up of lower Fae who had fled from the outskirts but among them were also some high Fae of both Seelie and UnSeelie descent. Nothing like a mass murderer on the loose to bring opposing sides together.

"I did figure out where Cheshire is being held, though," Alice continued, causing me to perk my head up.

"You did?"

"Yes. Though you aren't going to like it." She leaned back in her chair and pursed her lips.

"I don't particularly like anything right now. Just tell me." I already had an idea of where my mother was holding Chess, but I hadn't had anyone confirm it as of yet. Everyone had been pretty leery of me in general. When you pull a power play in a room full of people word gets out fast, and the word was to stay the fuck out of my way. Not like I was complaining, but it did make getting information harder.

"He's not in the dungeon—"

"Then he must be in the Hall of Mirrors," I interrupted. "Of course that nasty bitch would throw him there." I shook my head with a frown. "I don't know how she even managed it with the Shadow man prowling around, not unless she has some other way in then I know of."

"He's not there either." Alice shook her head, her blonde locks whipping around her face.

My brow scrunched down at her words. If he wasn't in the dungeon or the Hall of Mirrors where else could he be? While Chess and I might have had a falling out, it didn't mean I wanted him to rot somewhere. Knowing my mother, and how she felt about half-breeds, in general, there was no doubt that she had made wherever Chess was as horrid as possible.

Alice must have seen the distress on my face, because she placed her hand on top of mine and gave it a pat. "Don't worry we will save him, you'll see. You're the Queen of the Underground after all."

"I wish people would stop calling me that!" I spat out, irritation filling me. "One little show of power and everyone goes crazy. I can't even get it to happen again, at least not to that extent."

"Have you been practicing lately?" She cocked her head to the side.

I chewed on my lip before responding, "Kind of."

"Meaning not at all." Alice sighed and stood from the table. "You can't keep denying who you are forever. People are relying on you. *I* am relying on you." She placed her hand on her chest. "If you can't accept your powers and get them under control, who else is going to save Chess from the Bandersnatch?"

"Bandersnatch?" I sputtered. "But that is just a stupid monster made up by that asshole Lewis."

Alice shifted in her seat, uncomfortable by the mention of her ex-lover and my foul language. Though, living with me I would think she would be used to it by now.

"Not completely." She looked down at her feet now, not meeting my eyes.

"Alice." Her gaze snapped up at the commanding tone of my voice. "What does that mean?"

"While the Bandersnatch in his book isn't real. There really is a Bandersnatch in the Underground that is really real." She held her hands up gesturing as she talked.

"That makes no sense whatsoever." I shook my head. "It's either real or it isn't. It can't be both."

Alice placed her hands on her hips with a huff. "Stop thinking like a human. Not everything is so black and white as all that.

The Bandersnatch is not a thing, it's a place."

"Okay," I drew out. "Then where is this Bandersnatch?"

"In the Seelie Queen's bedroom, of course."

CHAPTER 2

SWITCHING SIDES

"WATCH WHERE YOU are swinging those!" Alice ducked as a vine swung out from the eggplant I was trying to maneuver around my backyard.

"Sorry." Gritting my teeth, I tried to focus on the wobbly, purple vegetable whose chicken legs were not sprouting fear in anyone's heart. "It's not as easy as it looks."

Apparently, controlling plant life when not in a life or death situation was much more of a daunting task than one would think. Just getting the eggplant to walk around the garden was more of a challenge than it should have been.

I had created one badass tree monster that had taken out a dozen guards. It couldn't be that hard to replicate, could it?

Focusing on the power surging out of me, I searched out the creature I had created, and directed it toward the vegetable's feet. It stopped chasing Alice only to swing its long vines and wrap them around her waist.

"Stop! Let me go," the blonde screeched, struggling to get out of the eggplant's tight grip. "Lady, tell it to stop!"

"I'm trying," I growled. With my eyes locked on the magic pouring out of me, I didn't hear the gasp that came from behind me until it was too late.

"Katherine. You're...you're one of them." My mother's voice caused me to lose my focus as my eyes jerked to her petrified face.

"Shit." The loss of concentration meant that my creature decided to take on a mind of its own and, for whatever reason, quickly began to spin in circles, swinging a screaming Alice with it.

"Hold on," I snapped and turned back to the rampaging vegetable.

Instead of redirecting the vegetable, I yanked my magic back from it, the green veins of magic quickly returned into my skin. Out of breath, I dropped onto the ground with a huff; leaving Alice sprawled out on the ground. As a half-breed, I was able to exert more power than most Fae, but it seemed like nowadays, even the smallest bit of magic wore me out and animating vegetation was no small feat.

"Maybe we should take a break?" Alice suggested, adjusting her hair while she dusted off her pants. When she saw we had company she stopped her fiddling and looked to me for guidance.

Standing from the ground, I didn't bother dusting off myself as I turned to my mother, who was frozen in place.

"Mom, what are you doing here?" I took a step toward her but stopped when she stepped back as well, fear filling her eyes.

She shook her head at me, one hand up and then in a blink of an eye that fear turned to anger, and she was stomping toward me. "Who are you? What have you done with my daughter?" My mother pointed a French manicured finger at my chest.

I shrugged. "Nowhere. I'm right here, where I've always been."

I probably could have tried to appease her more, tried harder to explain, but I was tired of hiding and even more tired of trying to explain myself to those closest to me.

Shouldn't she love me the way I am no matter what?

Her lips pursed together in a thin line as she looked at me and Alice, and then down to the creature that had shriveled back into a regular, old, eggplant. After a moment or two, her eyes narrowed back onto me.

"Don't think you can fool me, whoever you are. I know what I saw, and I won't be treated like an insolent child." She jerked her hand at the purple eggplant lying deserted on the ground.

"Mom, you are being silly." I crossed my arms over my chest and tapped my foot. "No one is treating you like a child."

"Don't call me that." She bared her teeth at me, snarling.

"Don't call you what?" I cocked my head to the side. "Silly?"

"Mom." My mother snapped at me, her eyes full of fire. "You are not my daughter. You have no right to call me that."

Taken aback by how viciously she had responded, I wasn't quite sure what to do. My mother had never shown me this side of her. I knew she could be as brutal as the rest of them when it came to something she wanted, but I had never been on the receiving end of it.

Not really able to help myself, I decide to poke the snake. "Well, if that's the case, I suppose I don't have to come to dinner anymore. Than Margery won't need me to call her. You know, since I'm not your daughter and all." I smirked and watched as my mother's face began to turn a kind of purple eggplant color from her rage. "I guess that also means that I can color my hair whatever I want, since you know, I'm not your daughter."

To prove my point, I let my magic ripple over me, changing my white blonde hair into a neon purple.

Picking up the ends of my hair to examine it, I glanced over at Alice. "What do you think? Does it suit me? Maybe I'll keep it like this when I go to the protest?" My mother gasped in horror as I tried not to grin. "You don't think anyone would care, do you? I mean, I'm not your daughter, so what I do doesn't affect you in any way."

Growling, my mother crossed her arms. "You've made your point."

"Have I?" I cocked my head to the side and waited. When she nodded, I let go of the glamour with a sigh. "I really didn't expect you to give in so fast, Mom. It's not like you."

She flinched when I called her mom again. Maybe she hadn't accepted me completely.

"Well," she snapped. "You gave me little choice, and besides, only my daughter would have the audacity to threaten me with purple hair. If you'd been an imposter you would be trying to appease me, not drive me into an early grave."

"Ah, Mom, that's so sweet." I clutched my heart in mock adoration.

"Don't start with me, Katherine." She narrowed her eyes, and then turned to Alice as if she had just noticed she was there. "I know you? You're that woman everyone's talking about. Gathering the creatures together. What was your name again?"

"Alice." The blonde Fae supplied, pressing her mouth into a thin line. She didn't seem to like my mother's reference to the creatures any more than I did.

"Yes, that's it." My mother nodded her head and then dismissed Alice as easily as she had started, turning back to me. "Really, Katherine. I don't understand what is happening at all. You're human. How can you even be one of them?" Her nose scrunched up in disgust, and her eyes strayed back to Alice, who glared, and crossed her arms over her chest.

I rubbed my temple and sighed. I didn't really want to get into the long complicated story that was my existence.

"Would you believe me if I said that there is Fae blood in our family?" I offered up, hoping it would satisfy her need to know the details.

"Nonsense." She sniffed. "There is no possible way that any of the Nottingtons would ever be with one of those creatures. We are pure."

"Are you sure about that?" I raised an eyebrow at her, ignoring the fact that her comment was as racist as they came. "Maybe grandmother, or one of the great-grandmothers had a Fae lover we don't know about."

My mother opened her mouth to protest, but then closed it with a snap as her brow crinkled. She must have thought of someone that was likely to have that kind of relationship and not tell anyone about it. But if she knew anything she wasn't telling. Her face smoothed out and a stern frown covered her features.

"Not that I am aware of. Anyways," she opened her handbag and pulled out a thin card, "I just came by to give you this. Since it will be a few weeks until you can get one of your own."

I reached out my hand and accepted the card, a little part of me danced with glee when I saw it was a debit card to the account we had talked about. I locked eyes with Alice, trying not to grin like a crazy person.

"Now that is for essentials, bills, food, and the like." My mother shot us a look. "*Not* for housing those creatures in your grandmother's house."

"Thanks, Mom." I went to hug her, but she held her hands up to ward me off.

"No hugs, dear. You are covered in dirt. Now that you have the card, I have to be going. I need to let Margery know that the Nottingtons will not be coming to the protest." She smoothed her hands down her outfit and gave an exasperated sigh. "I suppose I'll have to tell your father. Though, I have no doubt he will be more pleased than surprised. He always did like the strange and unusual. I'm sure he will want to talk to you about it. Do try and keep the theatrics to a minimum. Being one of them is one thing, but showing it off to the world is another. Besides, who knows what the government will decide in the next few months. You don't want to end up in some kind of lab being experimented on, do you?"

"Of course not, Mom." I nodded my head in agreement. I had no ambitions to tell the world of my new status. The fewer people who knew the better in my book. If the Seelie Queen had anything to say about it, I wouldn't be around much longer for it to matter.

That thought made my heart heavy and my eyes burn. I had the sudden urge to hug my mom but restrained myself. No need to make her worry more than she already was. I didn't even know if the spell really would kill me, or if it was just Chess being dramatic.

"All right. I'm off. It was good to meet you…Alice." She gave a small nod and left.

Alice eyed my mother's retreating back and turned to me with a frown. "We should probably stop for the day."

"That's probably a good idea." I sat on the back steps of my grandmother's house and sighed.

I'd been house sitting for her for a few months now, and there was still no sign that she would be back from her sabbatical in Florida. Not that I was in any hurry for her to return. There was still a gaping hole in her house that I hadn't even begun to figure out how to explain to a carpenter. I was lucky my mom had come around the opposite side of the house and not by my room. Or I would have had more than just a small fit to deal with.

"I'm sorry about your mother. Are you all right?" Alice slid down onto the step next to me in a move so graceful I would never have been able to pull it off.

"What do you mean?" I placed my head on my hand and angled my face toward her.

Her bright blue eyes squinted at me as if trying to figure me out. "Besides, your mother showing up you didn't seem like yourself today. Certainly less focused." She gestured to the abandoned eggplant on the other side of the garden.

"Just distracted is all." I sighed and dragged a hand through my hair.

"Thinking about Chess?"

"No!" I snapped and then frowned at the knowing look she gave me at my quick response. "I mean, not really. It's a lot of things." Mainly Chess. "Why should I care about him anyways? He certainly doesn't care about me."

"You can't just leave him there." Alice placed her hand on my arm, and I shrugged it off to stare hard at the ground.

It wasn't that I didn't want to save Chess. I did. My heart hurt just thinking about anything bad happening to him, but there was also another part of me that still ached from the words he had said.

Flattered. He had been flattered that I loved him. I was a good friend. Thinking about the words made my anger ignite all over again.

Had I been just some kind of sick game for him? See how long it took to get the Seelie Princess to fall for him before ripping her insides out and smashing them on the floor? If any other guy had done that to me I would say fuck them and be on my merry way, but the Bandersnatch...

"What exactly is the Bandersnatch?" I glanced at Alice out of the corner of my eye. "You said it's a place, right? What kind of place? And how is it in my mother's bedroom?"

"The how I can't help you with but the what..." She trailed off. "Well I don't really know what it is exactly either."

"Then how do you know anything about it to begin with? Carroll couldn't have made it all up in his head if he hadn't have heard at least part of it from you," I pointed out.

Alice stood from the stairs and began to pace. With her hands behind her back, her plaited blonde hair swung with every step she took. The dark charcoal of her pants and her light blue blouse made her seem like she had just come out of a business meeting and was ready to head back at any moment. It was weird how she had so easily let herself merge with the human world when she finally got out of her shell. Better than me for sure.

"Alice?" I stood up and placed a hand on her arm, halting her pacing. "What is it?"

She glanced up at me with sadness in her eyes. "I told Carroll of the Bandersnatch, it's true, but I was only trying to sound important. Like my adventures were more fantastical than they were. So, I may have told a fib or two to make him think the Bandersnatch was a creature, when I really don't know anything about it at all."

My brow scrunched down in confusion. "Then where did you even hear about it if you don't know anything about it? How do you know it's a place and not a creature?"

"The where I just learned from the group. But how I knew before?" She paused; several emotions crossed her face at once. I almost thought she wasn't going to answer before she began again.

"I really shouldn't. It's not my story to tell." The blonde chewed on her lip in an unladylike fashion that was out of character for her. "He would be so cross with me if I went back on my word. No I must, I can't, but you should know." She nodded her head at me; her train of thought seemed to be spiraling down a hole. "You really should. Maybe he could tell you then he would forgive me for even saying anything at all? But would he even want to see me?" She began pacing again, her hands reaching up to touch her hair. "I don't look like myself anymore, would he even recognize me?"

I grabbed a hold of her shoulders and turned her toward me. "Who Alice? Who?"

The blue of her eyes glistened as unshed tears threatened to fall. The anguish on her face was so heartbreaking I wished I hadn't asked. But I had to know.

When she finally answered me it was in a voice so quiet that I had to strain to hear her.

"Hatter."

CHAPTER 3

ALICE'S HEART

SITTING ON THE couch next to Alice in the living room, I pushed the box of Kleenex toward her. One thing I had learned about having the ex-human as a roommate was she was over dramatic and a bit emotional. With the way she was looking now, without even saying anything, meant crying was inevitable.

"Take a deep breath, it will make it easier." I patted the blonde on the back, trying my best to be comforting. I was getting tired of being the comforter; I wanted a bit of sympathy too. I was the one who was doomed.

"All right." Alice hiccupped and breathed in deep before letting it out. She turned to me with a small, wilting smile. "I think I'm ready to talk about it now."

"Good. So about the Bandersnatch," I started in.

"Oh no. I cannot tell you about that until you hear the whole story." Alice shook her head at me.

"The whole story?"

"Yes. How I came to the Underground in the first place. If you don't know how Hatter was before, you won't understand how he is now." Anguish filled her voice, and it made my heart hurt for her and Hatter. She clearly cared for him, even if she hadn't said as much.

"But didn't you tell Carroll your whole story? I've already read the book and so have you." I gestured to the book that was sitting on the coffee table in front of us.

When Alice first came to live with me I had been skeptical that she would be able to deal with being back in the human world. But she had surprised me time and time again. First with her weird obsession with reality shows, and then the one eighty she did when the fleeing Fae needed guidance. She didn't hesitate to step up and take charge. Sometimes I felt like she would be better off being the princess than I ever would be.

"Yes, I know all that. But like with the Bandersnatch, I didn't exactly tell the whole truth." She flipped her hair over her shoulder and her lips quirked up in a mischievous smile. "A woman has to have her secrets."

"Okay." My eyebrows rose at her statement, I wasn't sure I really wanted to know what really happened when she went to the Underground, but I didn't think I would be able to get the information I needed if I didn't let her do it her way. "So, what happened then?"

Alice sat up straighter on the couch and placed her hand primly in her lap as if she hadn't been torn to pieces at the thought of telling Hatter's secret. Being Fae had certainly made her more than a little mad.

"So, it is true that I fell down a rabbit hole chasing after a rabbit in a waistcoat. Of course, that didn't happen here where your hole is but over in England." She placed a finger up to her chin, tapping it. "And he wasn't really a rabbit now that I think about it but more like our friend Trip. He said his name was Watch, but I never did find out why he was named that. Do you suppose he is related to Trip?" She glanced at me in question. "Maybe we could ask him next time he comes by?"

"Maybe," I said simply not wanting to get too far off topic. "So, how old were you when you went to the Underground the first time?" I drew on my old memories, trying to place when I'd seen Alice before. "I think I only met you once or twice, and both times you were a different age, and the last time…" I trailed off not wanting to bring up old mistakes.

More polite than I could ever be, Alice ignored my reference and answered, "Ten, if I remember correctly. I had just snuck away from my nanny because she was being horrid. Who wants to spend the day learning arithmetic's when the weather was so lovely?"

"The thought," I agreed, letting my sarcasm bleed into my voice. I wouldn't need the weather as an excuse not to do math. The fact that I breathed air was reason enough for me.

"Exactly." She nodded her head. "So, you know the part about falling down the hole bit, and then the talking doorknob I made up, because really, how boring is it that there is a reception desk to the Underground?" Alice snorted, and I couldn't really argue with her.

The doors to the Underground sat in a world between worlds which was given the uncreative name of the Between. There you must sign in with Type and Gripe, the two-headed grumpy sisters that could quite literally bite your head off. There were even keys issued to those who wished to travel between worlds. It was all very civilized and modern, but nowadays it looked more like a battlefield than a way station.

The thought of the destroyed doors and what was left of the reception desk caused a shiver to slide down my spine. I wasn't looking forward to seeing the creatures behind that destruction again.

"So, the reception became a talking door. What else?" I sat back in my seat; I had a feeling this was going to take a while.

"Well, unlike the story I spun to Carroll, I actually ended up getting into the Underground by a talent that I'm not very proud of." She blushed and looked down at her clasped hands.

"What?" I sat up now, actually getting interested in her story.

"Pickpocketing," she muttered and blushed deeper. "I stole the key from the sisters all right. It was low and unkind, but they kept going on and on about needing a key and needing to sign in, so I just did it."

I couldn't help the little giggle that came out of me at her confession. Pickpocketing. Alice? It was hard to believe the prim and proper woman before me could do anything as childish as picking someone's pocket.

"It's not funny." Alice crossed her arms over her chest and pouted. "I've felt guilty about it ever since it happened, and I had hoped to apologize to the sisters and return their key, but you never gave it back to me, and now they are missing too!" She shot me a nasty look.

"Don't blame me." I pointed at my chest with a shake of my head. "I didn't lose the key, the dumb tree took it from me. I passed out and when I woke up, I was in the Seelie Palace; the key nowhere in sight."

Alice frowned, her brow scrunching together in thought. "I wonder where it went then."

"Probably still there at the bottom of the tree," I reasoned.

"Do you think so?" She pressed her fingertips to her mouth and stared hard at the coffee table. "If we could get back to the tree and get that key, then I could give it back to the sisters." She smiled at me as if I had answered all her prayers before a split second later her face crumbled. "But what does it matter if they are gone? And it's not like the key will do anything now anyways with the doors blasted to pieces. Oh, I'll never get to apologize now."

I shoved the box of Kleenex toward the blubbering Alice and sighed. Already crying and we weren't even to the good parts. I wondered if I still had some wine in the kitchen. Maybe if I plied her with enough alcohol she would be more comfortable. Though, if she was used to faerie wine, it could very well leave me as the only one intoxicated. At the moment, that certainly wasn't a bad thing.

"It's all right, Alice." I made soothing, shushing, noises at the crying Fae. "I'm sure you will find a way to pay them back just like you are trying to help Chess by telling me about Hatter."

I held my breath and hoped my subtle hint to try to veer her back on track would go unnoticed.

"Hatter?" She looked up from her tissue. "Oh yes, we were getting to that, weren't we?" She dabbed her eyes and blew her nose in a manner that made me force back a noise of disgust.

"So, I met so many creatures and amazing Fae, but none of them stood out quite like Hatter." Her eyes lit up with a happy sparkle. "He wasn't like the other Fae

I had met. All kinds of talking animals and beasts. Well, you know what I mean."

I nodded; I certainly knew what it was like. Brownies, two-headed birds, opalaughts, and Satyrs. The last made a small part of me quiver in fear, but I shook the thought away. I wasn't there anymore, and besides, I was a bad ass magical being now, I would never be anyone's victim again.

"So you only went to the UnSeelie Court?" I asked pushing my unpleasant memories to the back of my mind.

"Of course. Could you imagine your mother letting a human in her court?" She gave me a pointed look. "If I had stepped one foot in there she would have thrown me in the Hall of Mirrors a lot sooner."

"Something has been bugging me about that," I interrupted her from continuing. "If the Hall of Mirrors' entrance is in the Shadow's Between, and the doors are encased in iron, how does she get any of you in there? Only a half-breed could pass between the mirrors, and no one with Fae blood could touch the iron without getting burned. Not unless they had some kind of hazmat suit."

The image of the Seelie Queen, or some other High Fae dressed in a large yellow suit, made a small smile crawl onto my face.

"I don't know what a hazmat suit is but I do know how I got in there." She gave me a curious look.

"How?"

"There was a man. Or at least I think he was a man." She tilted her head to the side and seemed to think on it. "He was covered in black from head to toe in some kind of billowing cloak. He didn't talk, but he was tall and had a sort of ominous presence about him. He reminded me of those men who handle funerals?"

The man she described in conjecture with the conversation I had with my mother before, left no doubt in my mind that the man was the Reaper. No one but my mother and me knew anything about my mother's deal with the harbinger of death. There was no way it was a coincidence.

"So back to Hatter." I pushed the thought of the Reaper to the back of my mind to think on later, and focused on what I needed right now.

"Yes." Alice scooted forward in her seat at his name. "Hatter wasn't like the others. He didn't treat me like a child." She paused and a small smile crept up on her face. "He listened to me when I spoke, and talked to me like I was an equal, and not a lowly human. He..." she trailed off, her hand reaching up and touching her lips.

"Alice?" I smiled at the look on her face as she dropped her hand with a small blush. "Did something happen with Hatter?"

"What? Of course not." Alice ducked her head so I couldn't see her expression, though the red on her face seemed to spread from her cheeks to her neck.

"Do you like him?"

"Well, of course I like him. He is one of my dearest friends." She looked up from her lap, a sharp look in her eyes, daring me to contradict her.

I couldn't help but smirk at how obvious it was that she was hiding behind her friendship with Hatter. So that's why she was so worried about how he would react to her telling me.

"Then how is Hatter different now? How did the Bandersnatch change him?" I plied her for more information, hoping maybe I'd find out not just what I needed to know, but maybe she'd let something else slip about her own relationship with the stern-faced Fae.

A wave of sadness covered her face. "It's just terrible. It is like all of the light and joy was torn out of him. He doesn't laugh or play. Hatter won't talk about it, not even with me. He used to tell me everything too. My heart just doesn't reach his anymore."

Her voice broke and I patted her back as she began to cry once more. I had heard of criminals coming out if prison changed, but I'd never heard of a place literally tearing the light from them. Was that even possible? The Hatter I saw didn't seem like someone who had ever known a day of joy in his life, let alone be someone that Alice would love, and I had no doubt that she loved him. Though, a bitter part of me grumbled about her and Dorian when she had someone of her own.

"Do you think," she hiccupped, "He will ever be the same as before?"

I sighed. "I don't know. Some things take time. But the good thing is you're Fae! You have several lifetimes to get there," I pointed out with a smile.

"If the shadows don't kill us all first," she mumbled.

"Enough doom and gloom." Dropping my hands from her, I grabbed the remote and switched on the T.V. "Let's watch some baby mama tear a new one into some poor shmuck. Huh?"

She sniffed and wiped her nose, nodding.

We both turned to the television, but instead of screaming couples, we were looking at a breaking news report with the headline 'Aliens? Demons? Or something else?' A dark haired reporter stood in front of a crowd of people surrounding a podium where the president stood preparing to make a speech.

"I'm Amanda Newton, bringing you breaking news from the White House. The president himself will be answering our questions concerning the new rush of magical creatures, known as the Fae. However, the truth remains to be uncovered. Some say they are aliens from another planet, some radicals are calling them demons, but maybe they are something else altogether? We hope to find out now, here, at the White House."

The camera panned to the president as he addressed the crowd.

"The creatures known as Fae are here temporarily until their home can once more be called safe. They mean us no harm. We should welcome them with open arms. Anyone who is caught trying to abuse our visitors will be brought up on charges." The president glanced beside him to someone out of the cameras range; an adoring expression filled his face.

"Mr. President," a reporter called out from the crowd.

"Yes?" He pointed to them.

"What proof do you have that these Fae are not a threat and are not here to stay? How can the American people sleep at night knowing their families are safe with these creatures running around the country unopposed?"

Even though I was one of those Fae running around, I wanted to hear what the President had to say. Glancing over at Alice, I could see she was on the edge of her seat to know the answer to the reporter's question as well.

The president paused for a moment; he didn't seem to have an answer prepared for that question. Honestly, I didn't see any way that he could prove that we weren't a threat besides our words and actions. Though, since we hadn't started tearing apart the country, or tried to enslave the human race, I thought we were doing a pretty bang up job keeping our word.

The reporters didn't seem to think so, because the moment he paused, they began to shout questions at him. The president began to lose his cool and collected poker face.

"Well, I...um..." the president stumbled over his words and looked off to the side again, an expression of panic covering his face.

All of the reporters turned as well as did the camera to the person he was looking at.

The moment I saw that blonde head of hair and that familiar cocky smile, I jumped to my feet. "What the fuck!"

Dressed in a stylish, black business suit stood Gab. Her blonde hair was pulled back in a sophisticated twist, and she had a smile that would have melted even my panties had I been anywhere near her. The way the reporters' faces began to have a dreamy haze left no doubt that she was spewing a heavy amount of pheromones.

"That's illegal," Alice commented from my side.

"No shit." I snorted. "What the hell is she even doing there?"

"Shh. She's about to say something." Alice waved a hand at me and we turned back to the television.

"Hello," Gab addressed the crowd of adoring humans. "My name is Erydesa of the Seelie Court." She paused for a moment, her eyes sweeping the area. "My fellow Fae and I have been driven from our home and have sought shelter here in your world. The humans have always been kind to our people, and it is unfair of us to burden you so, but we desperately beg you to tolerate our existence in your world for a little while longer." Gab sniffled and then pulled a tissue from somewhere, dabbing her eyes, though I was sure there wasn't a tear in sight. "Once the threat to our world is gone, we will return as if we were never here in the first place. Thank you."

Gab stepped back from the podium as the reporters rushed her with questions. The security guards ushered her off the stage, and the president ended the conference.

Clicking the television off, I turned to Alice to ask her what she thought of this whole thing, but a voice from the hallway cut me off.

"Hello? Is this thing on?"

CHAPTER 4

A HELPING HAND

ALICE AND I glanced at each other. Shrugging her shoulders, she continued to pat her eyes dry, seeming to have no intention of getting up to see who it was.

"Don't worry, I'll get it." I rolled my eyes at her while getting up from the couch and making my way to the hallway.

Like most things in my grandmother's house, the hallway wasn't very big, but she had jam packed it with as many family pictures as she could fit on the tiny wall. In the center of the wall, surrounded by my sister's and mine school pictures, and some of my mother's wedding photos, was an old antique mirror.

The mirror was one of the first ones I had covered when I came back from the Underground. Square and about three feet tall, it had a brass frame in an ugly dark beige color. The mirror had always given me the creeps, even before I knew they could be used to travel between worlds.

"I don't think they can hear me, Pat." The voice said behind the sheet covering the surface. "Are you sure this is her house and I'm not in some basement?"

A cough like wheeze was followed by an irritated growl, "Of course, I'm sure! Don't you think I know my own devices? A millennia of creating mirror portals and this is the thanks I get?"

"Now, Pat, you know that's not what I meant." The voice changed to a soothing tone that I registered in my mind well. My Fae father had used that voice on my mother so many times I had lost count. Hearing it now had my hand reaching out to pull the sheet off the mirror to reveal his handsome, but strained face.

"Father?" I watched him with a growing curiosity. "What are you doing here?"

In the mirror stood the Seelie King. His blond hair was cut short and fell over his face, where worry lines marred his otherwise young and youthful face. Fae might not age quickly, but stress could kill them just as fast as any iron, and I could imagine the king was under a lot of stress lately.

"See. I told you I knew what I was doing." The other voice grouched at him, pulling his attention back to the mirror.

Startled, he jumped back, his dark brown eyes widening. "Ly—I mean Lady, or do you prefer Kat? I'm not quite sure what I'm supposed to call you." He gave me a sheepish grin and scratched the back of his head. The cream colored tunic he was wearing shifted, allowing a scar I hadn't seen before to be visible along his wrist.

I wanted to ask about it but thought better of it and smiled instead. "Kat's fine." My brow furrowed having thought of something. "What do you want me to call you? I mean, technically you are not my father. Do you have a preference?"

"Oh, uh." He fumbled for a bit, his face turning a slight pink color. "Whatever makes you comfortable, I suppose? You can call me father or you could call me king or your majesty..." he stopped and chuckled. "It is all kind of silly, isn't it? This whole no name rule."

I had to smile. I had almost forgotten what a goof ball my father was, nothing like my mother. I always wondered how they ever got together in the first place.

"I apologize, I don't usually use these confounded things. I'm a bit out of my depth I'm afraid." He gave a nervous laugh and glanced over at something off to the side. I could only assume it was the mysterious Pat who had been speaking earlier.

"That's all right," I assured him kind of awkwardly myself. "So, what brings you to my humble hallway?" I gestured around me laughing at my own stupid joke.

"Well, first off." He stood up straighter, his eyes surveying me as if he hadn't seen me in years. "I wanted to see how you were doing. I know we didn't really get a chance to talk the last couple of times you came to court. Though, some of that couldn't be helped."

The first time I had come to court as a human, I had no idea who he was, and was more focused on finding Hatter than getting cozy with the royals. Not to forget, I was drunk on faerie wine at the time too. The second time hadn't been any better.

When your mind is full of revenge, all thoughts of getting reacquainted with relatives are pushed to the back of your mind. All I could think about then was punishing my mother for what she did to Chess and making sure it didn't happen again. Finding out what her true intentions were was just an added benefit.

Shifting my weight from one foot to the other, I let sarcasm seep into my words. "Yeah, it's kind of hard to get reacquainted when you are fighting for your life."

"Fighting for your life?" he shook his head, confusion etching his face. "There was no such threat. No, your mother may be high strung and stubborn—"

Pat snorted off to the side. "That's an understatement."

"—as they come." he frowned. "But there was no way she would have ever hurt you."

I pursed my lips and stared at him hard. Not hurt me? Did hair pulling and siccing the guards on me not count? Maybe his definition of what counted as bodily harm had changed since I became human.

"I mean, not really," he stumbled over his words at my glare. After a moment he sighed. "You have to understand, Kat, your mother is under a lot of pressure. When you...passed, it was hard on all of us, not just the prince."

"So you thought it fit to punish him before you got all the facts and locked down the Underground? Yeah, that makes a lot of sense." I scoffed, my eyes looking off to the side as I crossed my arms over my chest. Should I be defending someone who was now friends with the bad guy?

"Now, you can't blame that all on her. You know we were all tricked, and what was she supposed to do when it looked like the man you were promised to caused your death because of his dalliances? Any parent or ruler would have done the same." He said the words, but his eyes told me he did blame her, at least to a certain degree.

When I had gone to the tree after I saw Dorian kissing Alice, the rest of the world hadn't known that it was all a trick, or that it hadn't really been his fault. Even I hadn't known what was really going on at the time. We were all just pawns in a game we didn't know the rules to. A game I was getting tired of playing.

"Anyways," I said, changing the subject from what was soon to be a full blown argument. "I'm sure you didn't come here to lecture me, so what do you want?"

"Ha! She's your daughter all right." Pat gaffed from out of sight, not being able to see the person who was talking was becoming really annoying.

"Would you be quiet?" my father growled, the first hint of irritation showing on his face, his head jerked to the side as he chastised the voice.

"Well, excuse me for breathing. Let me remind you, that you are in my home, not the other way around, your majesty." Pat, who was becoming more definitively male, snarled before the sound of footsteps stomped away.

"Who's Pat?" I couldn't hold back the question anymore. I couldn't remember ever meeting someone named Pat, certainly not someone who would talk to the Seelie King with such disrespect and get away with it.

"Oh, him?" he pointed a thumb toward the general direction Pat's voice had come from. "Just an old friend of the family, nothing to worry about. He's just a grumpy old man who needs to find more hobbies than fiddling with these silly mirrors."

"All right," I drew out accepting his answer, but not quite believing that was all there was to it.

"So, the reason I was calling is that I believe that it is high time I put my foot down." He puffed his chest out, and his arms shifted like he had placed his hands on his hips. "Your mother has gone too far, taking your boy and all." He shook his head and sighed. "We are in dark times, and you need all the help you can get. Taking Cheshire was just petty of her."

My heart lifted at the mention of Chess, and then crashed when I remembered where he was currently residing. Even though we had a falling out, I couldn't help but care if he was all right. I needed to know, not just to ease the guilt in my heart, but because a silly part of me still thought we might have a chance.

"Are you going to have him released, then?" My voice was hopeful and thankfully only had a bit of desperation in it.

He shook his head, his blond hair swaying slightly. "No, no. I can't do that. I don't have that kind of power, but you do." He pointed a finger at the mirror. "If anyone can release Cheshire from the bowels of the Bandersnatch it would be you."

"But how can I? I'm in the human world, remember?" I gestured to the room around me. "It's not like I can easily get back over there. The portal to your world is closed to me, and I wouldn't begin to know how to make a mirror active that wasn't already that way before. Believe me, I've tried."

The mirror in my room was completely smashed from when my Fae mother kidnapped Chess. I had gone to every thrift store I could find, looking for a full-length mirror that I could use to get back to the Underground, but no matter how much I tried, I could never get the mirror to activate. There had to be some kind of trick to make it a portal between worlds, I just wished I knew how.

"Ah." He held up a finger and then gestured off to the side to someone. "That is why I'm here."

A short man, with a head full of wild, peppered hair, stepped up and into the frame. His even larger ears only offset his large nose. He wore a set of goggles that he pulled down off his forehead to set over his eyes, and he squinted to get a good look at me.

"Pat here's talent is creating portals, he can make a portal out of anything with a reflective surface. He set up all of the mirrors in our world and made it possible for you and Chess to use them." My father stood behind Pat letting him take up most of the mirror.

"Nice to meet you." I smiled at him, he kind of reminded me of Mop in a way. Though, Mop had a thick accent and was a brownie, he and Pat seemed to be kindred spirits when it came to being just down right grumpy.

"Nice? Not really." Pat grimaced and nodded. "But it'll do."

"What will do?"

"The mirror of course. I haven't created a portal this small in a while, but I believe I still have what it takes to pull it off. Now, stand back and let me do my work." He cracked his knuckles and shook his shoulders as if ramping himself up to do something big.

"Wait! Now? You want me to come through now?" Panic filled my chest and my eyes searched around me as if there was something there that could help me.

"Of course, silly girl. Why else do you think we are here?" Pat rolled his eyes and looked behind him. "I thought you told me she was brave?"

"She is." My father pressed his lips together in a frown, and then an apologetic smile crossed his face as he glanced back to me. "I'm sorry this is such short notice, but really, the sooner you are over here the better. Time is really of the essence, and we can't wait for the Shadows to make their next move. Plus now is the best time, your mother is off visiting the UnSeelie Court, comforting the queen over her loss."

My heart clenched at the thought. Poor Mab, she lost her son because of me, and when she just got him back, lost him *again,* because of me. I wouldn't be surprised if that woman hated my guts. I certainly deserved it.

"Fine. I get your point," I cut him off and held a finger up. "Just hold on a second." I darted out of the hallway and into the living room where Alice sat munching away in front of the television. "Hey, Alice."

She glanced up from the TV, her hand pausing mid-bite. "Who was that?"

"My father has found us a way back into the Underground, but we have to get going now if we want to save Chess, and get out before my mother gets back from the UnSeelie Court." My hands moved in rapid flourish as I tried to get everything out in one breath. Taking a deep breath, I waved her over. "Are you coming?"

"No, I don't think so." She shook her head with a definitive movement. "There are plenty of Fae who need me here. I can't just take off whenever I feel like it."

Alice was starting to make me look bad. I was supposed to be the savior, and here I was only thinking about myself and getting

Chess out. I hadn't even thought about the other Fae here in the human realm.

While I saw her point, I really didn't want to go alone. Plus, if I had any chance of getting Chess out, it would be with her help. She knew about the Bandersnatch more than I did.

"But what about Hatter? Don't you want to see him again? I'm sure he would be happy to see you, especially now with Hare and them gone." I watched her to see if she would take the bait. One thing I had learned from my time with Alice and the Fae was if they didn't want to do what you wanted the first time around, make it all about them, then they were more than happy to pretend like it was their idea in the first place.

She seemed to think about it for a moment, and then without a word, rolled the bag of chips up, set them on the coffee table, and stood from the couch. Her sensible heels clicked on the floor as she walked across the room. Before she reached me, though, her dress pants and blouse were transformed into the blue and white dress I had first met her in, except less moth-eaten and stained.

"What?" she asked when I arched a brow at her. "I can't very well see Hatter dressed like that, he wouldn't even know how to react."

"I didn't say anything." I held my hands up and fought the smile that threatened to creep up my face. There was definitely something going on between those two, and I was bound and determined to figure it out before we left the Underground.

"Are you about finished?" Pat's voice called out from the hall. "We haven't got all day."

"We're coming, hold your horses." Coming around the corner, I stopped in front of the mirror once more, this time with Alice by my side. "We're here. Now what."

Pat's nose stuck up in the air as he looked down at us. "While you were dilly dallying, I already set up your mirror here to act as a portal from your house to my workshop."

"And where is that?" I craned my neck trying to see around the edges of the frame but could only see a few sets of shelves around my father and Pat's forms.

"In Summerville, of course, silly girl." He fiddled with some gadget with several gears and levers, only half paying us any mind. What kind of Fae was he? He couldn't be a Higher Fae; he wasn't tall enough or attractive enough. Most Lower Fae tended to be animals, or like in Mop's case, a brownie. I was about to ask, but Alice jumped in before I could.

"But Summerville is all the way on the other side of the Seelie Court," Alice whined, stomping her foot against the wooden floor. "How are we going to get to Cheshire in time?"

"Well, if you want to be that way." Pat reached up to the mirror his hand beginning to glow. "I can just take back my portal and you can just—"

"No!" Alice and I cried out in unison.

"I mean, no." I cleared my throat and glared at Alice. "Thank you. Summerville will be fine."

"That's what I thought." Pat sniffed, the glow on his hand dimming as he lowered it back down.

"All right, so…" I trailed off eyeing the mirror. "It would be difficult to just walk through it, but we could probably crawl through it on all fours or something. What do you think, Alice?"

"I'm not getting my clothes dirty." She crinkled her nose. "I know how often you clean these floors."

"Well, if someone else would help me with the chores they'd get done more often," I said between clenched teeth.

I swore if there was a list of the worst roommates ever, Alice would be number one, or at least in the top five. She didn't do chores. She didn't pick up after herself. I found chips all over the couch and floor every other day, and I was lucky my mom had given me money, or I'd have been eaten out of house and home within the next few days. With her figure, it was a wonder where it all went to, even Fae had to worry about getting fat, didn't they?

"You two are worse than a pair of rabid dogs. Just put the mirror on the floor." Pat waved his hand at it, impatience littering his voice. "Then you can just step into it."

Alice and I looked at each other and shrugged. I grabbed the mirror off the wall and carefully placed it on the floor. Sliding my hand along the edges to activate it, I stood up as I waited for the surface to ripple.

Standing by the frame, I gestured to Alice. "After you."

She took a step backward, a wary frown on her face. "It's your portal, you go."

"Fine." Taking a deep aggravated breath, I stepped into the swirling liquid. "Here we go again."

CHAPTER 5

PORTALS AND GADGETS

IT WAS WEIRD going through the mirror feet first. Instead of being fully engulfed in the cool liquid, it was a slow climb that started at my toes and crawled up my legs, like I was sinking into quicksand.

When I came out the other side, I ended up on a dusty floor in a heap of junk. My back ached and hands burned from being jabbed by random bits of metal. I turned around just in time to see Alice's feet coming for my head. I jumped to the side, so as not to get turned into a Kat pancake but fell into another pile of junk.

Really?

"Uck!" Alice lifted her arms, her nose crinkled up at the dirt coating her skin. "Don't you ever clean in here?" She shifted around in the pile, pulling out a corkscrew-like mechanism from behind her back.

"Who has the time?" Both our heads turned to look at Pat.

In person, Pat was even smaller than he was in the mirror. He barely reached my father's waist, and my dad was more than a foot taller than me. Pat wore a pair of overalls that had different tools hanging on a belt wrapped around his waist and random parts stuck out of every pocket. He had his goggles up on his forehead once more as he eyed us on the floor.

The Seelie King stood beside Pat, his hand behind his back looking as regal as any King could standing in the middle of a mountain of junk. His cream shirt fell over his muscular frame and landed just below the top of his matching pants that covered his plain shoes. Unlike the rest of the Underground, who was bound and determined to look obscene and sexual, his was more professional and inviting. Which I was thankful for honestly. If I had come in to see him in one of Chess', or God forbid one of Jewels' outfits, I would have needed some extensive therapy.

"Well, what are you waiting for?" Pat gestured at us, breaking my train of thought. "I didn't bring you here to take a nap on my floor. I have work to do, and so do you."

Easing up from the ground, my eyes scanned the room. Just like its owner, it was filled with different tools and gadgets. And mirrors. There were mirrors on every surface and wall, of every shape and size, some of them even without frames.

"So, you make all the portals in the Underground?" I stared in awe at the amount of mirrors surrounding us. "How?"

"What do you mean how?" he said it like it was the worst question I could have possibly asked. "How does anything magical work?"

Was that a rhetorical question?

"It just does." I shrugged, answering anyways.

"Exactly. So don't ask questions you already know the answer to." He sniffed and turned his back on us, going to a workstation to fiddle with a mirror he had separated into pieces.

"Speaking of glamours." My father stepped in. "You and..." he glanced to Alice and frowned. "I'm sorry. I don't think we have met."

"We have actually, but it was a long time ago, I'm not surprised you don't remember." Alice gave him a small curtsy; smiling at him with so much delight it was almost scary. "I'm Alice. Alice Liddell. Your wife had me imprisoned for your daughter's death."

"Oh my, that was you?" Horror covered his face, and he took a step back in surprise. It would have been funny had we not already been in a hurry. We didn't really have time to be rehashing old problems.

"Is that really important right now?" I stepped up between them, breaking the weird tension that had begun to fill the room. "Shouldn't we be going?"

"Yes, yes. You are quite right." He nodded, giving Alice one more cursory look before he turned to Pat. "Did you give them that thing?"

"Thing?" Pat's brow bunched together, and then he held a finger up and recognition filling his eyes. "Ah hah. That!" he went over to one of his shelves and dug around in a drawer.

The shelf he was searching was one of many shelves in the room. There was a multitude of them lining the walls where there weren't mirrors, each with some kind of gadget or a drawer full of items. Piles of glass from what could have been mirrors waiting to be put together sat on some of the shelves, and I couldn't help but wonder how much bad luck he had acquired over his years. He had to have smashed a few of them by now since he left them lying around like that.

After a moment or so, he turned back to us, blowing the dust off the surface of what looked like a small metal compact. "Here we are."

"What is it?" I took the item from him and turned it over in my hand before clicking the small metal latch, opening it up to reveal a mirror inside.

"It's a mirror, silly girl." He growled, shaking his head and muttering to himself.

"I can see that," I snapped back, closing the top of the compact with a click. "Why are you giving it to me? I can't exactly fit through the surface of it." The mirror was barely bigger than the palm of my hand, and I'd be lucky if I could fit a faerie through the frame let alone a grown person.

"I wouldn't expect you to. It's for communication, not transportation." He rolled his eyes like I should have known that as he moved across the room.

"So, then, how do I make it work?" I tapped my foot getting impatient with the way he was talking to me. If I wanted someone to talk down to me I could have stayed home with my human mother.

"Just like anything else in the Underground. You use your magic," my father spoke up, drawing our attention away from the grumpy Fae and to him. "This mirror will allow you to communicate to any mirror that has been activated as a portal."

"Really?" Alice asked, stepping close to me so she could see the compact in my hand. "Even between worlds?"

"Wouldn't be much good if it didn't now, would it?" Pat snorted from his place by one of the walls where he was messing with some of the mirrors on a shelf.

I stared down at the metal in my hand. Being able to speak between worlds could be handy, especially now that so many Fae were in the human world. I had better make sure to keep it close.

"You can use that to call here *if* you get into trouble. I can create a portal so you can get back here in a snap." Pat snapped his fingers and then narrowed his gaze. "But only *if* you are in trouble. Not because you are missing home or need something else petty like that. My powers aren't parlor tricks for your amusement. Though, some seem to forget that." His eyes slid to the king, accusation clear in his eyes.

"As I was saying before." My father stepped forward, ignoring Pat's glare. "You might want to think about using a glamour. Alice might cause a couple of curious glances but you," he pointed at my jeans and t-shirt, "You do nothing but scream human world. Plus, your mother has everyone on high alert looking for you. A full glamour wouldn't be a bad idea about now."

Pursing my lips, I looked at myself in one of the many mirrors around Pat's shop. I did kind of stick out. I thought about it for a moment, and then a slow smile crept up my face. I knew just what to do!

As my magic swept over me, my hair shortened into a fashionable bob, the color changing from white blonde to a light strawberry. The glamour on my eyes switched from green to a robin's egg blue and a sprinkle of freckles scattered across a newly elongated nose.

I slid my hands down my sides, taking in the dark brown leather pants that were tucked into knee high boots. The waist of the pants had a crisscross tie that was just barely hidden beneath the edge of my avocado colored spaghetti strap top that hung nicely over my A cup chest.

"Very nice indeed." Pat nodded in appreciation, his eyes scanning up and down my figure with a weird look that made me uncomfortable.

The look I had gone for was one I'd seen a friend from college use back in New York. The outfit was actually something Lydia had worn one night when we went to a frat party. I had always envied her small chest, and now I had the chance to try it out. Not needing a bra was a fucking fantastic relief!

"You're not one for being subtle are you?" Alice wrinkled her nose at me, her displeasure at my choice of outfit not even remotely hidden.

"If I'm going to pretend to be someone else I might as well go all out." I shrugged, an unapologetic smile on my face. "Now it's your turn. While I like the dress, there's no way anyone will believe you are just hanging out in the Seelie Court for no reason."

Frowning, Alice viewed her image in the mirror. Even though, I had just changed my own face I was still filled with awe when her hair flickered to a deep brown and her eyes became a darker shade that enveloped her pupil until it was practically nonexistent. Her cheekbones arched up higher on her face, and her lips changed from bow shaped, so top one was a bit fuller than the bottom.

Finally, her blue tea dress was morphed into a knee length, blood red sheath dress, and her black Mary Jane's were replaced with a low-heeled, strappy sandal. All in all, she looked good.

"Geez, Alice. Who did you use as your inspiration?" I cocked my head to the side, looking her over. She didn't look like anyone I had ever seen before, but the clothing was too close to that of something I had seen in the human world for her to have come up with it on her own.

"There was this woman on the television, who wore a dress like this. I have wanted to try it ever since." Her hands smoothed down the sides of the dress. She turned this way and that. She had a satisfied smile on her face as she admired her handy work.

"Well, good choice." I gave her a thumbs up, earning me a curious look in return. Turning back to Pat, I tossed the mirror back and forth between my hands. "So what now?"

"Be careful with that!" Pat jerked the mirror from my hands. "These things are fragile, you know."

"Sorry," I muttered while rubbing the back of my neck with a shrug.

Pat's furry eyebrows came together in the middle of his forehead, making them look like one big, long, caterpillar. I placed a hand over my mouth to keep from laughing as he berated me on the importance of taking care of things that didn't belong to me. Really, how could anyone keep a straight face with those eyebrows wiggling around like that?

"Are you listening, girl?"

I dropped my hand, swallowing a smile as I nodded at him. "Yes, I understand. I'll be more careful with it."

"You better be." He shoved the mirror back into my hands and then turned toward the front of the shop. "Now get out of my shop. I have things to do." He opened a door that chimed as it hit an old fashioned kind of bell hanging from the top of the frame.

"Wait." Alice stopped us before we could take a step. "Where are we going?"

I was glad Alice had asked, because my head was so out of sorts I would have walked right out the door without a clue of where to go next. At Alice's question, though, my father seemed a bit reluctant to answer. He shuffled his feet and looked around the room.

"Well, you see…" he trailed off scratching the back of his head, a gesture we seemed to have in common when we were nervous. "There's only a few ways into the palace that would get you in undetected."

"Then why can't we just use a mirror?" I directed my question toward Pat. He still had the door open and waiting for us with an impatient frown.

"You could do that," Pat started. "If you want to land right in the lap of the court guards."

Chewing on the inside of my cheek, I waited for my father to continue. If he didn't want to tell us where we were going, it probably wasn't anywhere I wanted to be. Not that I would know since the most I'd seen of the Seelie Court was the same as when I was the princess.

"Well?" I prompted him to continue. "Where are we going?"

He gave an unenthusiastic sigh before beginning, "You know your mother is being quite difficult as of late, and so she has tripled the guards as well as put the whole palace on high alert for the Shadows and you."

"Me?" I pointed at myself. I knew that people would be looking for me, but I had thought it was more because they wanted my help than because my mother was being a right bitch.

By the door, Pat gave a morbidly delighted chuckle. "Your little performance with the guards the last time has spread all over the court. It is making the people question the queen's ability to rule. If she can't even keep her own daughter in check, how is she going to keep us safe from the Shadows? It's no wonder she should have stepped down ages ago—"

"As I was saying," the king cut in, glowering at Pat. "You won't be able to just walk into the palace this time. You'll have to go through one of the lesser known entrances. That's why we brought you here, to Summerville. There is an entrance into the palace not far from here on Juba Drive that comes out into our library."

Our library he said it like it was still mine and his.

When I lived in the palace, the library was my one sanctuary that I could go to get away from my overbearing mother and the palace gossip. Father would frequently meet with me there. We'd spend hours there reading anything from the history of the Underground to mythical tales of heroes and heroines fighting evil and falling in love. It was one of our things, and the only time I felt like I was actually truly loved by at least one of my parents.

It was funny how I still loved the library in my human life. I guess some things never changed.

"So, we get to the library and then what?" I asked. "We just waltz into your bedroom? Won't we get caught?"

"No, once you get to the library you can take the mirror in there to the Memory room. That will at least get you half way. After that, you are on your own. I suggest keeping your glamour on until you make it to the room." He pulled out something from his pocket and handed it to me. "And this belongs to you I believe, it opens more than just the door to the Underground. It might come in handy."

It was a key. The one I had lost when I passed out at the glowing tree. But where did he get it?

"I found it," he answered my unasked question. "At the base of the tree you were found at. I had always liked that tree, and used to visit it from time to time before..." he trailed off his eyes going sad, and then just as quickly, his face smoothed over replaced with a small hopeful grin. "Well, that was before. Now it's a reminder that what is lost can always come back to you when you least expect it."

The smile he gave me made me feel like a little girl again, and all I wanted to do was be enfolded into his arms. Both the human and Fae part of me were daddy's girls and it seemed we both missed them.

Placing the pink ribbon around my neck and tucking the key into my shirt, I followed Alice to the door. I paused and turned back to my father who hadn't followed us.

"You aren't coming?" I frowned, disappointment filled my voice.

Guilt covered his face, but he didn't step forward to comfort me. "As much as I'd love to help you, dear. Your mother would have my head if she knew I helped you. King or not."

"I understand." I knew a little too well. He might have said before that she didn't have any intentions of hurting me, but I could tell we both knew that wasn't entirely true. If it suited her she could hurt just about anyone who got in her way.

"If you need anything just call on that mirror. Really anything at all. Don't worry about Pat. I'll take care of him." He stared hard at the older Fae, daring him to contradict him.

"Bah." Pat waved a hand at him and left the door, leaving me to catch it before it closed.

I stood in the doorway half in and half out of the shop, just taking him in. The thought of leaving him there didn't sit well with me. I couldn't help but feel like if I walked out this door I would never see him again. A burning sensation pricked at my eyes, and I forced myself to look away.

"Well, I guess I'll be going now," I said lamely, clearing my throat of the thick lump that had formed there. "Um, bye."

"Good-bye. Lynne." His words resonated with me as the door closed behind me.

CHAPTER 6

JUBA DRIVE

STANDING OUT IN front of the shop, the anxious feeling I had was briefly forgotten at the sight before me. Unlike the UnSeelie Court that was all gray stone, Summerville had a deep, rich, brown-red brick stone that lined the ground like a road. Pat's shop was made of the same stone, but more worn. The shop had gears sticking out of the walls, as if the wall had grown around them. A sign hung from the roof, and in sharp mechanical writing said: Pat's Portals and Gadgets.

The rest of the buildings were similar to Pat's. They seemed more like they had sprouted out of the red stone than to have been built. Each one of them was covered with their own unique style.

One that could have been a clothing store had huge scissors jutting out through the middle of the building. Another one had to be a coffee shop. While the building was made of the red brick, it was shaped like a cup with a handle, and I could have sworn there was steam coming from the top of it.

Did Fae even drink coffee? I'd never had it when I lived in the palace, never even heard of it. But then again, I wasn't allowed Faerie wine either, not until Dorian snuck me some one time. Thinking about that night made my face heat. It hadn't just been the first time I'd had wine, but also the first time we had kissed. Thinking about it now made me sad to know how much we had fallen apart. Where was he?

"What are you waiting for?" Alice jabbed me in the side, jerking me out of my thoughts. "It's not like you haven't been here before."

"I haven't."

"How is that even possible?" she flipped her brown hair over her shoulder and put her hands on her hips, looking very much the diva she was portraying. Alice made the skin she was wearing look natural and not at all like she was afraid her magic would slip at any moment. Not like me.

"I never left the palace before now." Shrugging, I moved away from Pat's shop and started down the road in the direction my father had instructed. I kept my eyes forward and tried to become invisible, even though the few Fae on the street were staring at us hardcore.

What are you looking at? Just some normal Fae walking down the street, nothing to see here!

"Well, that is complete rubbish." Alice scoffed catching up to me, not seeming to care that the locals were eyeballing us. "What is the point of being a princess, if you are confined to one place?"

"The kind whose mother was overprotective." I glanced around looking for the sign that would point us in the right direction. There were so many signs jutting out of walls and floors, each street name more unusual than the last. Cheaters Street. Wrong Way Lane. Liars Be Here Avenue. Were they trying to warn someone with these signs, or did someone just have a messed up sense of humor?

"Are you sure the queen was being overprotective and not just a nasty witch?"

A few Fae stopped to stare at us. I gave them a nervous smile and grabbed Alice by the arm and dragged her into the nearest alleyway.

"You probably shouldn't talk bad about her in her own court. You'll draw the wrong kind of attention." I kept my eyes on the entry to the alley, watching for anyone who would have followed us. No one did but several dared to sneak a peek in our direction as they passed by.

"Pfft. Like I care what any of these ninnies think. It's not like she can do anything to me anymore. The Shadow man is out and about now, there's nothing in the Hall of Mirrors to be afraid of." I slapped a hand over her mouth as her words got louder and louder.

"What the fuck is wrong with you?" I growled, hiding her with my body so that the onlookers couldn't see what I was saying.

Alice kept talking against my hand, trying to be heard over the muffling of my hand. In her glamoured form, she was almost a head taller than me, making it awkward with my hand so high above my head. When I didn't remove my hand, she jerked her arm out of mine and pointed at something behind me.

Turning around, my gaze trailed up to the sign she was pointing at. 'Loudmouth Alley.' I read. "Well, that explains it," I said to myself. "But why didn't it affect me?"

Alice gave me a 'you got to be kidding me' face. I didn't blame her. The question was pretty stupid. Nothing had affected me the same as the rest of the Fae, why should the magic on the streets be any different?

Grabbing her hand, I replaced mine with her own. "Keep that there until we get out of here, all right? We don't need any more attention drawn to us."

She nodded her hand firmly over her mouth and wrapped the other one around her waist as if to help keep quiet.

When we stepped out of the alley, most of the onlookers had gotten bored and had gone back to their business. Lucky for us, we weren't interesting enough to cause much of an alarm. I led the way back onto the street and resumed my search for Juba Drive. It was the only street name that wasn't named after something weird, not that Juba was in anyway normal.

After a moment or two of searching, I was jerked back by Alice's hand on my elbow. I turned to ask what the problem was when she pointed down a narrow path between two buildings. There was nothing lighting up the pathway, the walls surrounding it were broken down and neglected. At the entrance to the alley was a half-legible sign with its name handwritten in red paint.

Juba Drive.

"This must be it." I checked down each side of the street making sure no one was paying us any mind. I wouldn't want to get caught now after we made it this far. When I was sure no one was going to follow us, I gestured to Alice, and we made our way down the dark pathway.

"It's so dark," I stated after a few moments of walking with no light in the distance. It was just a bunch of pitch-dark nothingness. I reached my hands out in front of me to search for anything that could try to jump out at us.

When my hands touched a solid, rough surface that I assumed was a wall, I let my hand trail along it as a guide into the dark. We walked for a good five minutes or so with nothing but the wall as our hint to where we were going.

Alice tugged on the back of my shirt.

"You could use magic you know," Alice whispered next to me. Why she was whispering I didn't know, but it seemed like a good idea considering we didn't know if we were actually alone.

"Magic? I do plant life not balls of light," I reminded her. My footsteps became slower as I realized I could fall off a cliff and not even know it. What did she think I was some anime character that could shoot magic out of my hands at will? I was lucky I could do the things I could. Pushing it didn't seem like a good idea.

"When has that ever stopped you before?" she placed a hand on my shoulder stopping me in place.

She had a point. No matter the challenge, I always seemed to be able to do more than I should be able to. Why shouldn't I be able to conjure light out of thin air?

Turning around to where I thought we came before, I noticed the entrance was completely gone. We were in complete darkness now with no way to get back. There really wasn't a choice anymore. It was go forward and blindly hope we found our way or try to create a miracle.

"Here goes nothing," I mumbled, placing my hands in front of me. How the heck was I supposed to make light? Should I say some kind of magic word? Or was it as simple as my glamour and just thinking about it would make it happen?

"What are you doing?" Alice asked next to me, her hand still on my shirt, I assumed so as not to lose me, but I was happy to know I wasn't alone in here.

"Trying to make light, duh." I rolled my eyes, though I knew she couldn't see me.

"Oh, well, do you think you could hurry it up?" her voice was impatient and filled with just a hint of fear. Could good ole Alice be afraid of the dark? With what lived in here I wouldn't be surprised. I was afraid too.

"Do you want to do it?" I dropped my hands and glared in the direction Alice's voice came from. When she didn't answer, I put my hands back up. "That's what I thought."

I stared hard at where my hands were in the dark and thought for a moment this was silly. I couldn't make light appear out of thin air. It wasn't as easy as a snap of my fingers. Or was it?

Praying to whatever deity was listening, I placed my forefinger and middle finger together and snapped. The sound reverberated through the area, echoing off the walls we couldn't see and further into the distance. The sound settled and where my fingers were pressed together, a small ball of light emerged.

"You did it!" Alice jumped up and down in the dim light.

"I guess I did." I smiled at my accomplishment. Who said I couldn't make things out of thin air? Certainly, not this girl.

The light wasn't big, about the size of a regular light bulb, but it was enough to see a few feet around us, showing that we were no longer surrounded by red brick walls. In their place were dirt walls that curved overhead to create a cave like area. The ground was littered with rocks and debris; I wondered why I hadn't fallen flat on my face yet.

My victory was short-lived, though, because shortly after the light filled the cave, a scratching noise came from further in. Alice and I spun toward the sound. My little ball of light followed my gaze.

"What was that?" I squinted into the dark, trying to see further than the few feet the light provided.

Alice stepped next to me, her hand coming up to her face as she also tried to see what the noise was. "Should we investigate?"

Wasn't that the beginning of every horror film ever created? A noise in the dark, that for some unknown reason, the main characters decide it is a great idea to go find out what it is, usually, without a flashlight or any kind of protection.

But we weren't like those idiots. We weren't defenseless, and we weren't without a light. I didn't know if I could maintain the light and fight, but I sure as hell wasn't going to die in this cave. There were people depending on me. Chess was depending on me. Hell, I was depending on me!

"Oh my Lord," Alice stuttered, "It's...it's the JubJub!" Alice pointed at the shadow that had stepped close to the edge of my magically induced light.

"The what?"

Large talons clacked against the stone floor as a bird like creature stalked toward us. Its wings expanded out four feet in both directions, while its sharp beak snapped at us. Its bloodshot eyes bulged from its head, where its skeletal-like frame was covered with feathers that looked like they had been glued on rather than grown.

Alice grabbed me by the shoulders, giving me a little shake. "What the hell are you waiting for? Run!"

She didn't have to tell me twice. Turning on my heel, my feet pounded on the ground beneath us, each step causing a crunching noise. The little ball of light led the way, giving us just enough light not to trip over ourselves.

The JubJub chased after us. Its claws and wings scraped the ground and walls around us, causing the cave to shake and dirt to fall onto us. I kept my hands over my head, so as not to have an unexpected concussion, but my foot caught on a stone. I was thrown to the floor. A roar cried out behind me, and as I turned to look back, the ball of light followed my line of sight lighting up the cave behind us.

Gleaming red eyes bore into me, and for a moment, I was trapped. I couldn't think, couldn't speak. All I could do was listen to the rampaging beat of my heart as the JubJub came closer and closer...

"Ouch!" I jerked my eyes from the monstrous bird to glower at Alice who had stepped on my hand with one of her low-heeled boots.

"Don't look it in the eyes, you idiot!" her voice was a nasty snarl that I had never heard before.

Scrambling to my feet, I kept my eyes firmly planted in front of me and ignored the prickly feeling on the back of my neck telling me to look back. It wasn't just the Higher Fae who could ensnare humans, I couldn't imagine what kind of horrors it could wreak if it got into the human world. It made it that much more important for me to live so I'd never have to find out.

"Come on, this way." Alice tugged on my hand, leading me down a corridor that we hadn't been able to see before on the first time through.

As we made our way around the corner, the JubJub's steps became faster and more aggressive. It cried out as it bashed around the corner trying to get to us. The corridor was smaller than the other one, and I doubted the bird would be able to fit its whole body through the entrance with much ease.

Taking a chance, I peeked behind me to find the bird had indeed gotten stuck at the entrance, its wings too big to fit through. It clawed at the walls around it and tried to squeeze through. It cawed, a sound that made my blood run cold, and I had to force my feet to keep moving. Luckily, after a moment, it decided we weren't worth the trouble. It snarled at us and turned back the way it came. Or went to find another way.

An outcry from Alice had my vision jerking away from the JubJub and back to her, only I found myself alone. I searched the area but couldn't see her anywhere. We were still in the cave and the walls didn't really give any options for hiding. As I searched for her, I became more and more frustrated when there was just more and more wall in front, below, and above me.

"Alice? Where are you?" I took a step forward. My next words turned into a scream as the floor came out from under me.

CHAPTER 7

TICK TOCK

THE FALL SEEMED to go on forever. After the first five minutes I quit screaming. The hole was so big that I wasn't able to see the sides outside of my little ball of light that fought to keep up with my descent. I couldn't hear Alice's screams, meaning she had probably given up after a few minutes as well. Or she was dead.

I tried to not think about the last bit as I continued to fall further and further into the dark pit. My mind wandered to those who would miss me when I was gone. The amount of people on the list was kind of depressing.

The only one who would probably even care if I was gone were my human and Fae fathers. My sister might shed a tear or two but would get over it lieu of a new project. My human mother would do everything she was supposed to. Cry, wear black, and donate a huge amount to a charity under my name. But miss me? I wasn't so sure.

Then there was Dorian. Would he even realize I was gone? Or was he too far gone to see anything other than his own pain? I had hoped to be able to pull him out of the darkness he had fallen into, but when I was gone would there be anyone to save him. To save any of them.

The only other person who had an inkling of a chance of defeating the shadows was Chess, but he was trapped himself and couldn't help anyone. He definitely was not in any position to care whether or not I was alive, not like he would either way.

My train of thought was halted when my descent slowed. My vision began to clear, allowing me to see more than just darkness. The walls were becoming more prominent and visible.

Unlike the cave above, these walls weren't just made of dirt and stone. There was a carpet like material coating the walls in a black and white zigzag pattern that made my stomach lurch. Besides the nausea inducing walls, random furniture stuck out of the sides. Chairs and beds, night stands and full dining sets. All as neat as could be, like it wasn't unusual for them to be defying gravity.

The little ball of light I created began to flicker and die out as the hole grew brighter and filled with the overwhelming sound of ticking clocks. Just as the sound began to drive me insane, clocks of every shape and size appeared on the walls. Some coo coo clocks, some were old-fashioned grandfather clocks. All of them ticked incessantly.

"Lady!"

My eyes fell below me to where I could finally see the floor. Alice sat on top of a couch, waving her arm above her head. Finally!

As my feet touched the ground, I let out the breath I hadn't realized I'd been holding and looked back up. The hole I had come from had closed up, creating a ceiling of the same pattern with the furniture stuck to the surface.

"Where are we?" I wondered out loud as I looked around the room. It seemed like everything I had passed on the way down was now cluttered into a circular shaped room with no windows or doors. The room was a junk picker's fantasy, with more furniture than anyone could ever need, and more clocks than was sane.

"In my home."

Alice and I turned to where the voice came from. There was a table and set of chairs stuck to the side of the wall. A tea set with four cups and steam billowing from one of them sat on the table, not a drop spilled even at the angle. A fox like creature sat at the table that wasn't there the first time I had searched the room.

"You're lucky I had just sat down to tea and saw you, or I wouldn't have been able to slow down time enough to catch you. Then where would you be? Flat as a pancake on my living room floor." A tutting sound came from it, proving it was the fox indeed that had been talking.

Nine long fluffy tails swayed in the chair behind the fox that was sipping tea from a cup. A sapphire blue vest covered his dark orange fur, and he had a dark blue tie with a shiny gold pin wrapped around his neck. Black eyes twinkled at us as his lips — did foxes have lips —curled up in an amused grin as we gaped at him.

"Well, don't just stand there. I'm having tea, would you like some?" he gestured to the table with his teacup as if a talking fox was the most normal thing in the world.

"Um, excuse me," clearing my throat, I passed a look to Alice before shifting my weight from one foot to the other, wanting nothing more than to take my glamour off. "Thank you for saving us, but as much as we'd really like to stay and have tea with you, we have to be going. If you could just direct us toward the palace, we'll be on our way and out of your hair."

"The palace you say?" the fox asked, setting his cup down before him and crossing one leg over the other. The gesture was peculiar to see on a fox, even one larger than average size. "Why would you want to go to a place like that? Especially, at a time like now." He pulled a pocket watch from his vest and glanced down at the face before clucking his tongue. "Now is a not a good time to be at the palace. No matter the occasion."

"I understand that...uh...sir." Kill me now. "But we really don't have much choice in the matter. So, if you could just point the way..." I trailed off, waving Alice off before she could start to argue.

We didn't have time to get into theatrics, and every time she opened her mouth, we always ended up worse off. Not that I really had any room to talk, I'd gotten myself into my fair share of trouble because I couldn't keep my smart ass comments to myself.

"Tick. You may call me Tick." He answered, taking another sip from his cup using one hand as the pocket watch still ticked away in the other. The black lining of his lips curled around the edge of the cup, showing more finesse than one would suspect a fox to have.

"Really?" I couldn't suppress my amusement. You'd think I would be used to the weird names in the Underground after all this time, but every new one just made me want to giggle. I swallowed the urge to laugh, assuming he wouldn't appreciate it as much.

"Yes, really." His voice dared me to say another word about it before he snapped his watch closed. He slid from his chair and landed on the floor with more grace than any fox I'd ever seen. Tucking his pocket watch back into his vest, he approached Alice and me.

"As you can tell, I have a thing about time." He gestured to the clocks around the room, each one ticking their own little tune. "I keep the time here in the Underground and without me, the world as we know it would cease to exist."

Well, someone was full of themselves. The world would fall apart if he wasn't there to control the time? Like winding a clock was all that important. He could try fighting a whole horde of shadow Fae, and then we could talk about how important his job really was.

"That's really interesting." I tried to pretend to be interested in his job and not throttle him for wasting our time when all I really wanted was for him to shut up and tell us how to get out of here.

"Don't be smart." Tick wagged a finger at me, which was tipped with a long sharp claw. "I don't appreciate your sarcasm, nor do I have time for it, or you. So I suggest you forget about going to the palace and be on your way."

I exchanged a frustrated look with Alice, who urged me with a jerk of her head to keep trying. I was getting tired of having to convince people to help me. What happened to the good ol' days when people helped each other just for the sake of being nice?

"We would be happy to get the fuck out of your way if you would just tell us how." I was tired of playing nice, and if being polite wasn't going to help me, I'd do it the old fashioned way.

"I don't see how that is my problem." He sniffed and turned his back on us. He pulled a golden key from his pocket and stood on top of a chair to wind a clock with a mahogany finish and brass fixtures.

A growl rumbled low in my chest and my magic prickled along my skin as it bunched up in my stomach. I was this close to making this fox into my new fur coat.

"What if we made a deal?" Alice offered, placing a hand on my arm. She gave me a look that said 'calm the fuck down'. I glared at her but took a deep breath and let it out. The magic that had balled up inside me unwound and settled back where it belonged.

While Alice was right, I couldn't just blow our only way out of here to kingdom come, we didn't have time for any more bullshit. The last thing I wanted to do was make deals with unknown Fae. My previous deals had not gone well. One I was still avoiding, while the other had cost me twenty dollars worth of biscuits. No. A deal was not something I was eager to do.

"A deal?" the ears on his head twitched, giving away the interest he was trying to hide in his voice. He spun around, the key clutched in his claws. Tick jumped off the chair, placing his key back in his pocket as he approached us.

Oh no. This was not going to be good. Better beat him to the punch before I found myself on the wrong end of this arrangement.

"Fine. We can make a deal but within reason." I reached up to flip my hair over my shoulder but paused when I realized I was still glamoured and didn't have any hair to flip. Instead, I crossed my arms over my chest and tapped my foot. "What would be an acceptable trade for directions to the palace?"

The fox paced the room as he tapped a claw on his face. His brow furrowed as he thought about it. The sight of a fox pacing would have been funny enough a sight, but the fact that he was in a vest and tie made it hilarious. I must have given away my thoughts because Alice jabbed me in the side with a warning glare.

"I will do you one better." Tick stopped pacing and came to stand in front of us, keeping his hands held behind his back as he stood before us. "I will personally lead you to the palace if you can answer a riddle."

"A riddle?" My lips turned down in a frown. I didn't like the sound of that. "And if we get it wrong?"

The fox shrugged a gesture that should have looked awkward, but he somehow made it look natural. "Then you have to stay here as my guest for a hundred years. It gets awfully boring here all on my own and you two look like you could be entertaining." His tongue sneaked out to swipe across his jaw as his eyes leered at us.

A shiver ran down my spine. Too many animal-like creatures had given me that look lately, and it always left me wondering if they were thinking about food or sex. I couldn't decide which one was worse, bestiality or being eaten alive? The real question was did I really want to know?

"Agreed," Alice announced before I could say one way or the other.

Grabbing Alice by the elbow, I dragged her a bit away from the fox and snarled, "What the hell are you doing? You can't just agree to something like that!"

"But a hundred years is nothing." She cocked her head at me, her glamoured hair falling in a curtain over her shoulder. "Besides, I doubt any riddle he could give would be hard, he's too cute." Alice waved a little hand at him with a smile. Tick wasted no time grinning back at her, an eager gleam in his eyes.

"To you maybe. But I'm still human." I growled and then dragged a hand through my hair, yanking on the short ends, wishing for the glamour to be off and done with. "In a hundred years I will be dead! Then who will save the Underground?"

"Oh." Her lower lip popped out in a pout as if she hadn't thought that her actions could affect everything we both held dear. We couldn't just do what we wanted all willy-nilly. Fuck! I could just strangle her right now.

"While your conversation is quite interesting," Tick stepped in, drawing our attention back to him. "The young lady has already agreed and thus the deal can begin." His eyes and the anxious movements of his hands as they fidgeted behind his back said there was more to it than he was letting on.

"All right, let's get this over with," I muttered and then pointed a finger at him with a growl. "But I'm not doing a blood oath. I don't need your help that badly."

"No, no, no." he shook his paws in front of him. "I wouldn't dream of asking such a deal." Tick placed one pawed hand behind his back and used the other to cover his mouth as he cleared his throat. "Here is your riddle. Now think wisely before you answer because there are no do-overs."

No do-overs my ass, I wanted to say but kept my mouth shut as he began to speak once more.

"I am never silent but have no mouth. I couldn't shake your hand though I have two. A body I have but not a mind. I cry every hour, though I feel no pain. What am I?"

I was dumbstruck. That was his riddle? How stupid was he? There were so many around us, why would he use something that was right in front of our faces as the answer? I mean, even an imbecile could figure out the answer was a —

"Baby!"

That was the final straw. I was going to kill her. I didn't care if she knew about the Bandersnatch; she was too much of an idiot to be helpful right now. It would have been better for everyone if she had just stayed at home.

Anger swirled in my stomach, and I had to force the crackling of my magic along my skin to calm down. Now was not the time to lose control, no matter how much I wanted to unleash all kinds of hell on her.

"The answer is not a baby." My voice was low and dangerous, portraying exactly how much I was straining to keep my magic in check.

"It's not?" the innocent bewilderment on her face proved she didn't know how close she was to being plant food.

"Then what is your answer, dear?" the fox watched me, an impatient bored look on his face as if he didn't care one way or the other if I answered the riddle right. But I wasn't fooled, and I wouldn't be wrong.

"A clock. The answer is a clock." I shot daggers at Alice, who still looked confused. Why was I surprised? This was a girl who got easily tricked by the shadows.

"Is that your final answer?" Tick's lips curled up in a mysterious smile like he knew something we didn't. His tails whipped back and forth behind him with just as much enthusiasm.

"Yes, that's my answer." My voice was confident and not at all uncertain. Good for me.

"You are right!" he cried out, startling me at his sudden outburst. He grabbed my hand in his paw, shaking my hand with quick jerky motions. "Well done. In all my years as timekeeper, no one has been able to answer the riddle correctly."

"Great," I withdrew my hand from his clutches, trying to discreetly wipe it off on my pants. "Well then, I answered your riddle, let's get going."

"Quite right." He turned away from me and pulled out the key he had used to wind the clock before he stepped up to a floor length grandfather clock. Sticking the key into a keyhole on the glass door on the front of the clock, he turned the key and the door opened with a click. Holding the door open, he turned back to us, gesturing us in.

"Thanks." I moved toward the door, waving a hand over my shoulder for Alice to follow. "Let's get out of here." Before I could step into the clock, he held his hand up, stopping Alice in place.

"No, no, no." he waved his paws with a shake of his head. "You can go, she stays." Tick pointed a claw to me and then to Alice.

"But we got it right!"

"No, you got it right." He shook his head not even trying to hide the glee on his face. "She didn't."

My hands gripped my short locks in frustration. It wasn't fair. They kept changing the rules! At this rate, we'd never get to Chess before my mother got back from visiting Mab.

Maybe that was my problem. I kept expecting them to play fair. They're Fae, they didn't have the same rules as humans and even humans would screw you over if you let them. It was time I started thinking more like a Fae and less like a human.

"Fine. How about double or nothing?"

He tapped his chin with his claw, thinking on it and then waved his arms in front of him with a jerk of his head. "No, I already have her I don't see anything in it for me." His eyes lingered on Alice's glamoured form, a little too long for my liking.

"Fine." I snapped drawing his attention back to me. "If you get it right we both stay, if you get it wrong we both get to go."

Tick's eyes widened and then a broad smile covered his face. "That's more like it." He leaned against the clock's side, crossing one foot over the other. "All right then, what is—"

"No," I cut him off. "You answer my riddle this time."

Frowning, Tick stood up straight, no longer seeming so relaxed and certain he would win. Good. I held all the cards this time and I didn't intend to lose.

"Go on then. What riddle do you have for me? I will have to warn you, though I have never been beaten. So, don't think you can beat me with something short and simple."

I held back a snort and suppressed the urge to roll my eyes. Short and simple, huh? Let's see what he thinks of this one.

"What is black and white but red all over?"

He didn't even hesitate to answer. The fox was so sure of his answer. "A Cerberus."

"A what?"

Alice jumped in, disappointment filling her voice. "A Cerberus is a large three headed dog –like creature that is red with black and white spots."

I was pretty sure they were insane. No way, they were thinking the same creature I was thinking about. In Greek mythology, Cerberus was the guard dog of the Underworld and while it was indeed a three-headed dog, there was nowhere that said it was red with black and white spots. That would just be ridiculous.

"See! I'm right now you both have to stay." Tick slammed the door to the clock shut with a snap, not caring if it broke or not. He stalked toward us, his body shimmering as his eyes bore into us like he was wondering what we tasted like. I'm sure I was delicious, but I wasn't about to let him figure that out.

"Actually, you're wrong." I smirked, stopping him in his tracks. It was a strange sort of satisfaction that filled my chest at telling someone who thought they knew everything they were wrong. It was almost as good as bunnies and rocky road ice cream. Almost.

"What? Wrong?" his body stopped shimmering. He shook his head like it was the most ludicrous thing he had ever heard. "I'm never wrong."

"Ah, but you are." I didn't even try to hide the joy in my voice; I was so giddy I could have skipped. I wouldn't but I could have.

"If it is not a Cerberus then what the blazes is it?" he threw his arms up in the air, his irritation at possibly being wrong seeming to build in his voice.

"The answer is a newspaper."

"A newspaper?" he looked between us, bewilderment replacing his irritation. "What's that?"

"It's a paper you use to read the news. There are plenty of them in the human world."

"You cheated. You can't use riddles from different worlds."

"Ah, but you never specified that at the beginning of the agreement." I was feeling pretty proud of myself right then. "Now, we held up our end, it's your turn to hold up yours."

Anger covered his face, and then he adjusted his vest, his mouth forming a thin line along his jaw. "Very well, you win this one. Just give me a moment to change."

The glimmering along his fur formed again and unlike a glamour that poured over us in a blink of an eye his transformation was a bit different. His legs and arms elongated. His fur flattened over to show smooth muscle beneath. His tail disappeared and his hair fell down to his waist in a long, fiery wave of orange. The ears on his head were traded out for pointed, Higher Fae ears and his muzzle was replaced with a strong jaw line and lips that made me want to bite them. He was still wearing his blue vest and tie, but now it seemed more obscene than adorable and luckily —or not so luckily, he had formed a pair of loose fitting pants on his lower half. The only cute thing about him now was his bare feet that wiggled on the carpet.

"If you look like this why stay in a fox form?" Alice asked, appreciation for his new look filling her eyes.

I couldn't blame her. The fox named Tick was quite a fox himself. Suddenly, I had the urge to call a redo. Staying here with him didn't seem like such a bad deal.

"That is my form, but those at the palace prefer my human one. Not all my kind can change like this, you know. Only those who have reached their hundredth birthday can." He adjusted his tie and then he flipped his hair over his shoulder. "*I* have just celebrated my two hundred and fifth birthday. Changing form is nothing for someone like me."

"Well, good for you." I stopped gawking enough to put a little sass in my voice. "But we are kind of on a schedule, so if you wouldn't mind."

"Always in a hurry and so rude. Is she always like this?" He gave Alice a curious look and then when he caught her staring winked at her, making her giggle like a little school girl.

"Worse."

CHAPTER 8

LOSING CONTROL

THE INSIDE OF the clock was not any different than the rest of the cave above. It was dark and covered with rough dirt walls. Thankfully, this time we didn't have to rely on my magic to find where we were going. Tick had a whole light system set up along the sides of the cave, so that he could easily direct us further in. I just wished he would spend a little more time directing and a little less time flirting with Alice.

She had seemed to find a whole new liking to Tick in his new form. So much so that she continued to flirt and giggle as if we weren't on our way to the Queen's castle.

"So, why do you live down here?" Alice asked, walking beside the fox with her arms looped through his. He had become more of a gentleman once he realized he had been bested and couldn't do anything about it. Some people know how to lose gracefully, some don't. I was the latter.

"It's not like it was my choice." He snorted, sweeping his hands elaborately around us. "This would not be my first choice in homes if I had my way."

"Then why don't you move?"

I trailed behind them, letting them have their little moment. It wasn't every day that Alice got to meet someone who didn't want to blame her for everything. But since she still had the glamour on, we really didn't know if he would be accepting of her or not. If he had been down here this whole time, he might not even know who she was or care.

"I would, darling, but it's my job." He patted her hand, with a sullen sigh. "Part of the job description requires me to be secluded from the outside world. The JubJub bird is supposed to keep visitors out." He glared at me over his shoulder. "Bad things can happen when people think they can mess with my clocks."

"What's so special about them? They just keep time." I thought back to his room full of clocks and wondered what mysterious power they had that required a guard bird like the JubJub.

"They are not just clocks!" Tick halted our procession, dropping Alice's arm and turning to me. "I will have you know that I have a very important job, one that requires dedication and sacrifice. Not just anyone can be in charge of time. It is a difficult task that doesn't allow for much outside interference. The fact that I am even taking time away from my duties to take you to the palace could have exponential consequences. Did you ever think of that?"

He gnashed his teeth at me, rage building on his face, and I felt my own anger respond, which in turn, caused my magic to flare to life.

"I'll have you know." I stalked toward him, shoving a finger at his chest. "While you may be the keeper of time, there are other people in this world that are doing just as important tasks." I felt a sense of satisfaction as each poke to his chest, caused him to step backward. "Ones that require far more sacrifice than having to spend all of eternity winding damn clocks. Do you know how much pressure comes with being the savior? How many times I've wanted to just forget it all happened and turn my back on this place?" I waved my hands around me, the magic in my veins fueling my anger to extraordinary heights. It was like all the built up fear and denial had finally come to its tipping point and was spilling out all at once.

"Savior?" Tick stuttered, his eyes full of fear as he glanced at Alice and me. "You're the savior? The Seelie Princess reincarnate?"

"What the hell have I been saying the last few minutes?" I threw my hands up in the air with a growl. My powers leaked out, causing the ground to shake around us. "Haven't you heard? I'm dangerous." I moved in close until our noses were almost touching. "I'm a loose cannon just waiting to go off."

"But you're a half-breed." The moment the words left his mouth he realized his mistake, and he scrambled back from me, but there was nowhere to go. He was literally backed against a wall and at my mercy.

The power within me begged to be released, and instead of forcing it back down, I let it. I let it pour into the floor around me. Bright green plant life spread across the cave and up the walls. Vines shot out from around the fox and wrapped around his body until he was trapped, unable to move let alone speak.

But it wasn't enough. He thought he knew pain? Sacrifice? I wanted him to feel what it was like to be the only one to save the worlds. The only one that was powerful enough to stop the Shadows. The claustrophobic feeling of being crushed on all sides that consumed me every night until all I dreamed about was ending it all.

Tick cried out as the vines squeezed him. His eyes filled with such utter terror, like he knew he was going to die and there was nothing he could do about it. The bad thing was I didn't care.

"Stop." Alice appeared next to me, her voice slow as if not to spook me. She placed her hand on my arm. "You are going to bring the whole cave down on top of us, and we still need him to get us into the palace. You can't kill him, not now." She rubbed my arm with soothing motions that only served to irritate me rather than soothe me.

I shrugged her hand off and spun on my heel. As I marched away from them, I pulled my magic with me, and the sound of Tick gasping for air sounded from behind me. Ignoring them, I headed toward the direction Tick had been leading us as I tried to get a grip on my anger and the never ending need to destroy something.

Being the savior wasn't something I asked for. Hell, I hadn't even wanted to be on the school council in high school, being in charge of things had never been something I was good at. I was more of a do my own thing kind of girl, not a 'let's be sure everyone else is alive and enjoying themselves'. It took major self-control just to keep my mouth shut and not tell them all to fuck off half the time, not that I didn't let it slip out every once in a while.

Each step I took caused the ground to shake and small plant life to creep out of the dirt floor. I couldn't seem to control my magic now that the floodgate had been opened. My heart was pounding in my ears, and I couldn't even hear if Alice and Tick were following behind me. If I was more in my right mind I would have stopped to check, but my only thoughts were to keep moving so I didn't completely break down.

The path Tick had been leading us down didn't have any turns or forks. It went straight through the cave and ended at a dead end. Except it wasn't a dead end. On the wall was a full-length mirror, not unlike those seen around the palace.

"Uh...Lady?" Alice's hesitant voice reached out to me. My eyes searched for her through the mirror's surface and waited for her to continue. "Your glamour is gone."

Startled by her statement, my gaze fixated on my reflection.

She was right. In the midst of my fit, the glamour I had so meticulously held in place had melted away leaving me in my true form. Even the green of my eyes had been burned away and replaced with the raging blue of my Fae eyes.

The face that reflected back at me, terrified me more than the Shadows, more than losing Chess to the Bandersnatch, and more than death itself. The face looking back at me, while still my human face, made me frighteningly similar to the Seelie Queen.

It was like a punch to the stomach that caused all my anger to cool. My magic fizzled out and stopped sprouting around me. The icy glow to my eyes became just eyes again and sadness filled my heart.

What was I becoming? I wasn't like her. I didn't use my powers against others because I could. The Fae in me had been more than less dormant. Allowing me to have the best of being a magical creature without getting too power hungry. It seemed like the longer I was in the Underground the more I was losing control of myself, and I couldn't have that.

Swallowing my despair, I turned to the two and almost cried at the looks on their face. I had put that fear there. It was me who had been this close to terrorizing them, just because I couldn't control myself.

"I'm sorry, I shouldn't have done that." Hugging my arms close, I chewed on my lip, my anger replaced with uncertainty.

"You should be!" Tick shouted, and then snapped his mouth shut as if afraid of what I would do for his outburst.

"Stop, please." Sighing, I ran a hand through my hair, giving it a satisfying tug. It was so much better to be in my own skin with my own hair again. "I don't want you to be afraid of me. That wasn't supposed to happen."

"What did happen, Lady?" Alice took a hesitant step forward, her glamour still in place, making the look on her face hard to decipher. "I've never seen you lose control like that."

"It's happened before." My frown deepened as I remember the first time it happened.

It was the first time I'd had dinner with my family in a long time, and of course, that meant my mother was going to ride my ass the whole night. Luckily, Chess was there to act as a buffer, but that didn't keep her from poking at sensitive subjects. When I lost my temper, my human body was still getting used to my powers, and couldn't control the rush of magic that came with my anger.

The feeling of magic pouring out of me and into the earth, of creating new life just from myself was an overwhelming drunk feeling. I had felt invincible, like I could do anything. But magic had a cost, and if Chess hadn't been there, I might have burned myself out completely. Maybe even died.

Alice being here might not have had the same effect as Chess, but she did keep me from killing not only me, but also someone else. I had to get a grip on myself, or I wouldn't make it to the Shadows in one piece.

Shaking off the thoughts, I turned to Alice, "You might as well get rid of your glamour, Alice. The gig, as they say, is up." I giggled at my own little joke, though it was kind of a pathetic attempt to lighten the mood.

"If you say so." Alice pursed her lips and let her glamour go, revealing her normally blonde hair and blue dress. It seemed she was dead set on seeing Hatter again while dressed like her old self. Oh well, it was her thing, not mine.

"So then, Tick." I turned to the mirror in front of me once more. "I'm assuming this is the entrance into the palace?"

"Yes." His voice was stronger now, less fearful, but still cautious.

Ignoring the need to reassure him, I reached up to activate the mirror. My hand almost touched the frame when I stopped and spun around, my eyes narrowing on the fox.

"If you use a mirror to get into the palace, how do you activate it? You aren't a half-breed."

Alice's eyes moved to Tick as well. There was something wrong, and it smelled like a fox.

"Well, you see…uh…" he stumbled over his words, his hands wringing in front of him. "The thing is…" his answer was cut off when his eyes darted to something behind me, he then pulled his watch out of his pocket and tapped the glass. "Oh look at the time. I must be getting back now. Bye!" Before I could stop him, he transformed back into a fox and darted back the way we came.

"What the hell was that about?" I asked Alice who was staring at something behind me with fear in her eyes. "Alice, what is it? What are you looking at?" My head turned to find what she was looking at only to be caught in the icy glare of the Seelie Queen.

"Daughter, how nice to see you again."

CHAPTER 9

COMPROMISE

THE SEELIE QUEEN stood in the frame of the mirror, an amused, but sharp stare protruding through the surface. Her white gown clung to her curves, almost translucent in the library's light. It showed me more of my mother than I ever wanted to see. Her long white hair, the same shade as mine was piled on her head in a series of braids that gave the illusion of a crown.

She wasn't alone in the library. At her back were at least half a dozen guards, all armed with their golden armor and shiny swords. They stood menacingly, waiting for her command. I wondered if they remembered what happened the last time they came up against me.

When my eyes scanned across them, a few of them flinched, and I tried not to smile. Good. They remembered.

"Hello, Mother." No need to be rude right off the bat. "We weren't expecting you back so soon. We had hoped to surprise you."

"Well, my dear cousin needed to be alone so I came rushing back here the moment I found out you were coming. You know your father isn't very good at keeping secrets." Her smile was nasty while her words were playing the polite game.

"I hope you weren't too cross with him?" The warning in my voice was clear. She better not have hurt him or there would be hell to pay.

"Worried for your father now? You didn't seem so the last time you were here." She laughed and then placed a finger to her chin. "In fact, you didn't seem to care about anyone but yourself and that half-breed. Now, why is that, I wonder?"

Sighing, I chanced a look at Alice who was cowering behind me. She seemed to be trying to make herself as small as possible. She wasn't going to be any help as long as the queen was around. I might have instilled fear into the guards, but my mother still held the crown of Queen Bitch.

"The fox was yours I take it?" I chose to ignore her previous question, knowing that anything I said would just drive me into a deeper hole than I was already in.

"All Fae are mine, Daughter." The implication in her voice that said even you was not lost on me. My nails bit into my hands as I tightened my fists to restrain my need to correct her. I ground my teeth together to keep from saying something that would set her off.

"I am not here to argue or fight, Mother. I want him back."

"Who?" she pretended like she didn't know what I was talking about for a moment, and then shook her head with a secret smile. "Oh, that feline. I don't know why, he has done nothing but string you along, and then the moment you declared your love for him, he broke your heart. I would be a bad mother if I didn't punish those who hurt my little girl."

I fought back the laugh that threatened to come from my throat. Take care of those who hurt me? She was doing a bang up job on her own.

"But I'm not a little girl anymore. I can take care of myself." I tried to reason with her, no longer wanting to play the game I started.

"That remains to be seen." She sniffed and looked down at me with disapproval in her eyes. "Anyways, I'm tired of standing in this drafty library, come through and we can discuss this like civilized adults."

She was being nice. Too nice. There had to be something she wanted, or something she was planning.

My lips twisted in an unpleasant grimace before I reached up to touch the frame. Alice's hand stopped me before I could activate it.

"What is it?" I lowered my hand and turned to her.

"What if it's a trap?" she whispered, her eyes darting to the glass and back. "I'm still a fugitive, remember? What if it's just a trap to throw me back in that cell? I won't want to go back there, I won't!"

I hadn't thought of Alice's position in the Underground, or what making her come with me would mean. I grabbed her hand in mine and gave my attention back to my mother, who wasn't even pretending not to be eavesdropping on us.

"Before I come through, I need to make a deal."

"Oh?" her eyes lit up in a way that I knew nothing good would come from. "A deal? That's new. I'm assuming this has to do with the little faker?"

I winced at the title Alice had earned from her wish. While Alice might be Fae now, she wasn't always, and being magically endowed by a tree wasn't something that the born Fae were very fond of. Being Fae wasn't something you could just buy, and that was pretty much exactly what she had done. It didn't win her any fans, not that her tricking Dorian helped her cause any.

"I need you to promise not to hurt Alice or put her back in that Hall of Mirrors. It wasn't her fault she was tricked."

"But it is her fault that my darling girl got her heart broken." Her eyes shot an icy laser at Alice, who cringed and cowered beside me. "She had to be punished."

"Fine. She was punished. Now it's done."

"But what do I get in return? Pardoning a criminal is a high price, and I require equal payment."

"And what would be suitable payment for the life of one of your citizens?" Regret instantly formed in my throat at my question. I had opened myself up to whatever she wanted in return. I could only hope whatever she wanted was something I was willing to give.

She didn't even think about it. The moment I asked the question she was talking again, "I want your word that you will not try to take the Seelie throne until the time that I step down."

Of course she would want something worth more than what we were trading for, though it was only worth more to her than to me. She had made it clear where her thoughts were, and she found me a threat to her power. Well, she could keep her stinking throne and all that went with it. I didn't want it. Not that I was going to tell her that.

"I have a condition to add to that trade." I cleared my throat and tried to sound as superior as possible. "If you are to stay on the throne, I believe it is only fair that a council of your peers — not selected by you, but by the people," I continued before she could say anything, "To have final say in all major decision concerning the court and its citizens." Her mouth opened to protest, but I held a hand up. "It's a reasonable request seeing as how you caused this whole mess with the Shadows in the first place by making such decisions on your own."

Her eyebrows furrowed and a gnashing frown distorted her face. She wasn't happy with my condition, but the fact that she was thinking about it said that she knew I was right. But the question was would she do what was right, or would her pride get in the way?

After what seemed like hours, she finally threw up her hands in defeat. "Fine. I agree to your conditions. We will hold elections after this whole Shadows ordeal is dealt with. Agreed?"

I thought about it for a moment. Was there a way she could get around this? Had I messed up in some way? If the council was elected and not appointed by her then it would be less likely that she would be able to sway them to her way of thinking by bribery or threats. There really wasn't much else I could do to keep her in line without taking the throne myself. And I so did not want to do that.

"Well, what are you waiting for? Do you not wish to save your beau?" A twinge of irritation pinched her face, and she showed the first signs of being nervous by fussing with her skirt.

"No, I'm coming." My eyes met Alice's anxious face one last time before I reached my hand back up to touch the edge of the mirror.

The moment my hand touched the frame the familiar ripple coasted across the surface, activating the magic that Pat had no doubt put there. I took Alice's hand in mine giving it a tight squeeze, though I wasn't sure if it was more to reassure me or her. I think we both needed a little bit of comfort at this point.

When Alice and I stepped through the mirror and landed on the other side, I knew instantly something was wrong. The smile on my mother's face was just too happy for shit not to be hitting the fan. My question was answered when the guards circled Alice and me, their swords at the ready.

"What's going on?" I kept my eyes on the guards, my body tense and ready for whatever they might throw at us. I wasn't too worried, last time she had thrown more guards than this at me, and I took them all out without a sweat. But I had also been high on rage at the time, right now all I felt was uncertainty.

"I'm not doing anything, dear." The laugh that came out of her was wicked and full of self-satisfaction.

I glanced from the guards to her pale white face. "Then call your goons off."

"Goons?"

This time when she laughed it was like tinkling bells with an edge. It shivered along my arms and down my spine. It wasn't a pleasant feeling.

"You heard her boys, back off."

At her orders, the guards lowered their weapons but didn't move. They stayed circled around Alice and me, their eyes locked on us like we were going to attack them at any moment. If I had time for it I probably would have.

Deciding to ignore the little show she was putting on, I turned to her, my face deadly serious. "I'm here. Now can we please discuss Chess?"

"You are just no fun." My mother gave an overdramatic sigh, her hands holding up her dress as she approached me, circling me like the vulture she was. "Unlike, the half-breed. He used to be a lot of fun. Though, he still is in a different kind of way." A secretive smile covered her face and it made me sick to my stomach.

Had she and Chess? Had they? I couldn't even imagine it. My stomach rolled and I felt like I was going to be sick.

"Are you all right? You are looking a bit pale." She smoothed a hand along my back, patting it like the doting mother she wasn't.

The feel of it along my spine made my skin crawl, and I did everything in my power not to jerk away from her.

"You." She pointed a finger at the guard who'd had fear in his eyes when I looked at him. "Go get us something to drink and a cool cloth and bring it to my room. My daughter is feeling ill and we must make sure she is well taken care of."

Turning back to me, she placed a hand on my face and I let her. "Come, let us retire to my boudoir and we can discuss this unhealthy obsession with that ridiculous cat."

She looped her arm through mine and led me toward the library door. I walked with her until I noticed that Alice was not following. She was still by the mirror with guards all around her.

"Wait." I planted my feet on the floor causing her to stop in her tracks. "What about Alice? She needs to come too."

"But whatever for?" she cocked her head to the side, a questioning frown on her face. "She can't help you save the cat. There is no reason why she needs to be present at all. She'll be fine, my guards will be sure she is taken care of. Besides," She hugged me close to her and whispered gently, "We haven't had mother-daughter time in a long time. I think we are passed due, don't you?" she smiled at me ending her words with a high-pitched lilt.

Did I really want to have mother-daughter time with the Seelie Queen? No. Did I believe for one minute that Alice would be safe with the guards? Hell, no. But did I really have a choice?

Alice in a moment of courage I would never have expected from her spoke out, "Go ahead, Lady. I'll be fine." She placed her hands on her hips, giving the guards a haughty glare. "These bullies don't frighten me." I half expected her to stick her tongue out at them, but she didn't, and just did her best to seem as intimidating as possible for a girl in a powder blue tea dress. Good for her. She was more mature than me.

"See, all is well." she placed a hand on my lower back, driving me back toward the library door and leaving poor Alice lost in a wonder of men.

I HADN'T BEEN to my parent's room in like, well, ever. We weren't that close of a family, and besides meals and the occasional visit from my father in the library, I didn't really see them that often. My mother, as most could tell, was not exactly the maternal type, and I sure as hell didn't come running to her when I was scared or hurt. I had a nanny for that.

It was funny how my human life had been painted in almost the exact same way as my Fae one. Except for the arranged marriage and the dying. Those I was happy to not have written into my second life.

A servant opened large doubled doors, decorated with golden vines and leaves. The servant kept its eyes down when the queen passed but snuck a look at me when my mother wasn't looking. Unable to help myself, I gave the servant a wink, causing them to startle and blush.

I kept our encounter quiet and made my face stay neutral as I entered the room. I wouldn't want her to think I was having too much fun, or she might do something really atrocious. Not that the threats to mine and my friends' lives weren't already bad enough.

The room we entered had to be the sitting room, because there was only a sofa, colored in a deep red with matching armchairs and a coffee table in between. The red was the color of dried blood, making the room less welcoming and more like a crime scene. Apparently, the white and gold décor wasn't something she cared for either.

The walls were just as bad, colored in a bright red that seemed to drip down the surface as if it was a living being and bleeding. I kept away from the furniture and walls and let out a breath of relief when she didn't linger in the room. She went straight for a door on the right side of the room.

There was another door on the left side that was either a bathroom or something else altogether. It might have been my father's room. I wasn't sure if they were still sleeping in the same room or not. If I were him, I wouldn't want to breathe, let alone sleep in the same room as her. She might get into my dreams, or worse, my nightmares.

"Here we are." She twirled around, her arms and skirt spinning around with her. "This is more like it." She finished her rotation and let herself fall onto the bed with as much grace as a falling angel. Her skirts spread around her on the black duvet, making her dress stand out like a beacon on a dark night.

I searched around the room for somewhere to sit but there was only the bed, a couple nightstands, and one of those wooden standing closets. I sure as hell wasn't going to sit on the bed with her, so I stood.

"Now, daughter." She leaned back on her arms and threw one leg over the other as if posing for a camera. "Tell me. Why would you risk coming here for a half-breed? A half-breed, who not only doesn't return your feelings, but threw them back in your face."

"I need him." I didn't ask how she knew what happened between Chess and me. There were plenty of ways she could have found out. I wouldn't put it past her to have spies watching me all the time. I could only hope it was spies and not that she tortured it out of Chess.

"Yes, you said that already. But why? Why do you need him?" Her fingers tapped out a tune unknown to me on the bed, her face intently focused on mine.

"Like how you need father."

The way her face scrunched up at the thought of needing my father answered the question I had been wondering for a while. She didn't need him. She probably didn't even love him. He was probably just the right guy for the job, like how she thought Dorian was the right guy for me.

"I love him," I tried again.

"So? He doesn't love you."

I sighed, suddenly feeling tired. How do you explain love to someone who has probably never felt it in their life? It occurred to me then that I felt bad for her. I didn't know how old she was, but considering we could pretty much live forever, she had to be close to a thousand. A thousand years and never knowing love? Unimaginable.

"It doesn't matter if he loves me or not. I can't let him rot for not loving me."

"Well, that is just ridiculous. Of course you can. You are a princess and the savior. You can do whatever you want." She sat up on the bed, placing her hands delicately on her knees as she watched me. "For instance, if you wanted a hundred lovers you could have them like that." She snapped her fingers together, the sound of it reverberated through the room and three men popped into existence, each shirtless and attractive enough to make even a nun drool.

My mother gestured toward me, and the men turned their heated eyes my way. Each of them stalked upon me like I was prey ready to be devoured. I put my hands up in front of me and shook my head.

"No, I'm good." I gave them a weak smile, hoping it would deter them. It didn't. They circled around me, their hands going to my waist, my hair, and my hands. I tried to brush their hands off, but they were persistent in their caresses. "Not that you guys aren't hot as hell, but I'm really a one man kind of girl and — would you stop it!" I shouted out sending a shot of magic out along my skin when one of their hands got too close to my nethers for comfort. The shock of my magic made their hands drop away and I could breathe again.

"Get rid of them," I demanded, a crackling green energy hovered over my skin, the only thing keeping the men from trying to paw at me again.

"Very well." my mother sighed, disappointment in her voice. She snapped her fingers again, and I was blessedly alone again. "If you don't want a lover, I don't understand how you could risk your life for the half-breed. He isn't that great in bed."

"Let me put it into words that you will understand then." I held my hands up letting her see the magic that still hadn't been called back. "I need Chess. I want him and I want him now. If not for my own feelings but for the sake of the Shadows."

"The Shadows?"

I rolled my eyes. "What are you going to do if I fail? Who is going to take them on then?" When her lips pursed into a tight frown, I knew I was getting to her. "If something happens to me, he is your best bet to beat them, and he can't do that from inside the Bandersnatch."

"Fine. You may have your cat." She waved her arm, and the doors of her wardrobe opened. The moment it did the room felt colder. Darker.

I inched toward the closet. On one of the doors hung a mirror. The mirror was the length of the door and didn't have a frame. The surface of it was black and did not reflect anything back. It was like a void sucking in all the light and happiness in the world. I could feel it trying to get its claws into me as I stood near it.

I kept my eyes on the surface of the mirror as I held my hand up. This wasn't the first time I had encountered a mirror so dark, so full of evil. I doubted it would be the last.

When my hand touched the surface it wasn't solid, but it wasn't like the other mirrors. This one didn't ripple along the surface, and when I pulled my hand back it let go with a suctioned pop!

"A warning, daughter." My mother's voice called out behind me, and I didn't turn away from the mirror to answer her. "Those who enter the Bandersnatch don't come out. Ever."

"I'll get out," I said with more confidence than I had. "I have to."

CHAPTER 10

BANDERSNATCH

IT WAS LIKE trying to fight my way through one of those goopy toys kids play with, the kind that was wet and left a smelly rubber residue on your hands afterward. It filled every orifice until I felt like I was suffocating in black ooze. It seemed to last forever until suddenly it stopped. I popped out the other side as if it had finally had enough of me.

The other side wasn't any better. The air was thick, making it hard to breathe. Since there was no light it made the overpowering feeling worse.

I stood there for a moment, getting used to the pressure on my lungs. There was a sudden urge to run and an overwhelming need to panic that crept its way into my heart. It wasn't the darkness that was getting to me but the silence.

There was nothing. No wind. No background noise. All I could hear was the pounding of my own heart, and that wasn't a sound I would want to spend eternity listening to.

"Hello!" I called out, not moving from my spot in the darkness. "Chess?"

There was no answer.

Not getting anywhere standing here, I took a cautious step forward. Then another. The floor didn't give out on me, and nothing grabbed at me, so I kept going. I walked through the darkness, not knowing where I was going, or what was out there. It terrified me.

After what felt like hours of walking, I finally heard something. Voices. Or more specifically, yelling.

"You are nothing!"

"A leech."

"Worthless. Pathetic excuse for a Fae."

The insults just got worse and came from different voices. As I got closer I could hear something else, something underneath the nasty words that was muffled and strained.

It sounded like...crying?

I was almost on top of the voices now and the darkness had peeled back like worn paint to reveal a dim corner. In the corner surrounded by floating heads was a small child.

He couldn't have been older than five or six. His face was covered in dirt but there were trails of white running down his cheek from his tears. His hands pressed down on the ears on his head, that even in the dim light were distinctly stripped. A tail was tucked between his legs and his body was shaking in its place.

"Chess?"

My voice caused the child to look up from where he was trying to ball himself into the corner. Bright green eyes full of fear and despair looked back at me without a hint of recognition.

"Go away!" he yelled, his hands up as if to ward me off. "Leave me alone."

My foot paused mid-air, not sure what my course of action should be. He didn't seem to know who I was, and his appearance proved there was more than simple magic at play.

"Hey." I knelt down on the ground and scooted toward him, trying to seem as harmless as possible. "I'm not going to hurt you. I'm here to help you."

"No, you aren't! You aren't real. You're just a trick to mess with my mind." He shoved his hands back over his ears; the voices grew louder as if to drown out my words. "You aren't real. You aren't real," he muttered over and over to himself while rocking in the corner.

My heart broke for him. Was this what the Bandersnatch was? Instead of physically torturing you it played on your fears and ate at you until you went insane. I'd rather have had a bullet to the brain.

When I reached his side, I placed a hand on his head. He yelped and flinched away from me, his head shooting up to look at me with terror in his eyes.

"Please don't hurt me. I'll be good. I promise!" his words broke as he began to cry again, and I couldn't stand it anymore.

I wrapped my arm around him drawing him in against me. He struggled against my hold for a moment and then seemed to relax into my embrace. I let him cry and rocked him, making soothing noises in the back of my throat. The entire time the voices around us roared up into a deafening scream.

Getting a headache and quite literally fed up, I pulled on my magic until it warmed me. Chess stiffened in my embrace but didn't pull away. When I built enough energy up, I turned my head toward the floating heads.

"Silence!" my voice echoed through the darkness, and the power behind it quieted their voices. The heads just floated there now, not making a sound. "Don't you have something else to do besides torture a poor child?"

The heads actually exchanged a look before one of them, an older gentleman, opened his mouth to say, "No. Not really. It's our job." He seemed to shrug, though he had no shoulders. "And that is no more a child than you are, that is just what is left of the sinner."

"What are you?" I asked, pulling Chess closer to me when a few of them leered down at him. I didn't care if he wasn't a child, they had reverted him back to his child form and that was good enough for me.

There was always something worse about torturing a child. Like some kind of internal instinct that made you want to protect them. Of course, this child had been naked and rolling around in my sheets with me a week ago, and had quite thoroughly broken my heart, but that didn't make it any better.

"We are the Bandersnatch," the leader of the heads explained. "We serve justice to those who have sinned. And this child, as you so see him as, has sinned oh so very much." A delighted shrill filled his voice. "There is so much wickedness there we are almost full up on it. Not that we could ever be full." He shared a chuckle with his fellow floating heads.

I stared down at the child in my arms. Wicked? Chess was a lot of things. Womanizer. Liar. Cheat. But wicked? I didn't think so. I would know if I loved someone that evil. Wouldn't I?

Turning back to the heads, I asked, "Then why not let him go? You have had your fill. There is no reason to keep him here any longer."

"Ah," another one of the heads, a young woman spoke up this time. "But we can't, you see. The queen gave him to us to punish and we must punish, we must."

The way her eyes zeroed in on Chess had me pulling him so tightly to my chest that he squeaked. Loosening my grip on him, I focused on the leader. "It was the queen who sent me here to retrieve him. He was wrongfully imprisoned and must now be set free."

A gasp from the heads filled the room, and then they were talking at once. The air in the room became thicker as the heads bobbed back and forth, each trying to speak over the other.

"Quiet!" the leader called out, causing the other heads to abruptly pause. His dark eyes locked onto me, and it took all I had not to gulp at the intensity of his gaze. "There has never been a case where we have been wrong. He is evil and was given to us, thus we will not let him go. Queen or not."

"So you would defy your queen?" I asked a cautious edge to my voice. I didn't know what they would do if I kept pressing them, but I wasn't about to just leave Chess here now that I had him.

"What will she do? Punish us?" the heads shared a laugh before the leader's face sobered, this time when he spoke his voice shook the space, and I felt his words down to my bones, "We are the Bandersnatch, the thing of nightmares. Your fear is our food and no one —not even a queen, can stop us."

Chess whimpered and buried his head further into my chest. As always, my mind immediately went to an inappropriate place, and I found that if he had been in full form we would be in quite a compromising position. The sounds of his distress made me chide my own thoughts. Child or not, he still had a child-like mentality, and I shouldn't be thinking such things. The Bandersnatch, on the other hand, was messing with the wrong girl.

"You may be the thing of nightmares but you don't scare me." I stood from the ground, bringing Chess up with me. His small hands clung to my leg and his tail came out from between his thighs to wrap around my calf.

The laugh that came from the heads caused Chess and me to cringe. It was dark and full of power. The sound of it seemed to ignite something in the room, causing the scene around us to change. We were no longer in the complete darkness but in the Mushroom City, and standing before me was the blackened mirror leading to the Shadow's Between.

"We have touched your mind and know what you fear." The leader circled around us, his cronies following his lead.

This was their big power? Using glamours was something I knew about and the scene before me was a shit job at one if I had ever seen it. A scoff came out of me before I could think about it.

"You laugh?" he shouted his face turning a reddish purple. "We have brought you to the source of your fear and instead of quivering in terror you laugh, why?"

"First off," I gestured around the area, trying to keep my smile to a minimum, "You suck at glamours. A four-year-old could change the scenery easily. Secondly," I held up two fingers, "Come on, really? Out of all the things I'm afraid of you pick this?"

A giggle came from the feline wrapped around my thigh, his tiny face looked up to me with a small smile. Good. At least, he wasn't crying anymore. I placed my hand on his head, smoothing the hair between his ears and returning his grin with one of my own.

Chess' laughter must have really pissed the heads off, because they began to spin faster and faster around us. Their voices came out in unison, "We will teach you the meaning of fear, girl!"

Instead of being smart and preparing for their attack, I yelled back, "Give me your best shot!"

The Mushroom City melted away and in its place was a white empty room. The sudden change of lighting made my eyes hurt, and I squinted until they adjusted. The heads were no longer in sight, their voices were gone and the air lighter than before.

"Are they gone?" Chess let go of my leg, but he kept a hand on the edge of my clothing.

I waited, my eyes searching the room. They wouldn't have left so suddenly for no reason. It had to be a trick of some kind.

After a moment or so with nothing happening, I reached down and grasped Chess' hand in mine. "Keep close to me, and no matter what happens, don't let go of my hand." With a nod of his head, he tightened his grip on my hand.

The room was empty of any furniture or windows but there was a door. One dark red door stood out against the white walls. Well, if that wasn't ominous then I didn't know what was.

They wanted us to go through the door. They expected it. I hated doing what was expected of me, but at the moment, I didn't really have much of a choice.

Taking a deep breath, I let it out and glanced down at Chess. "Ready? Then let's get the hell out of here."

We made our way across the white room and toward the red door. Each step we took was harder than the last. The door seemed to pulsate in its frame. It bulged out toward us like it was a living, breathing thing. A whimper came from Chess, and I was jerked back as he stopped.

"What is it?" the pure terror on his face caused my insides to ache.

"I don't want to go." His voice was tiny and his words shook.

I had the sudden urge to pull him into my arms again and never let go. God forbid he asked anything of me in this form. A child form of Chess was a hard thing to say no to. It made me wonder if our children would look just as adorable.

Our children? I started. Where the hell did that come from? He didn't even want to be my boyfriend, what made me think he would want to have children with me?

The frown that had formed on my face must have seemed angry, because Chess began to back away from the door and me. I held my hands up and slowly approached him.

"No, no. Hey. It's okay. I'm not mad." I reached out to him and dropped to one knee. "I was just thinking of something unpleasant. It's all right."

He hesitated, his eyes on my hand and then to the breathing door behind us. Visibly swallowing, he seemed to decide that I was the lesser of two evils and came back to my side. His hand firmly clasped in mine, he let me lead him back to the door and hopefully to our way out.

Before I could place a hand on the doorknob, the door blasted open, throwing us back a few paces. Getting up from the ground, I grabbed Chess and pushed him behind me, my attention primarily on the open doorway. Then the smoke started.

Black, wispy trundles slowly built into a large billowing cloud that covered the surface of the room. No. Not yet. Not now. I wasn't ready. Fear started in my belly, making its way up my throat and choking me as I fell to my knees. Chess held onto me, crying and shaking me as if it would snap me out of it.

I knew that smoke, what lived inside of it. Avoiding it had been a pass time for me that was so familiar when the time came to come face to face to the being behind it I wasn't sure I would be able to stand up to it let alone beat it.

Nothing followed the smoke, and I realized something, it wasn't real. Just like the Mushroom City, it was just an illusion. The real Shadows were with Dorian, doing God knows what, and wouldn't waste their time with theatrics such as this.

Suddenly, I could breathe again. The fear dissipated and, with it, the smoke. I brought myself to my feet and took a deep breath in.

"Sorry about that." I gave a weak smile to Chess before picking him up into my arms. No more playing around. It was time to get out of here and nothing else was going to stop me, least of all a Goddamn illusion.

With a newfound determination, I crossed the room and didn't stop until I was out the door and into the dark. Unlike before though, I had a plan.

I snapped my fingers and called up my magic, the sound echoed in the dark. A ball of light that grew bigger and bigger lit up the area, showing us the mirror entrance not even ten feet away. Of course, as soon as we made our way toward the mirror, the heads reappeared.

"What do you think you are doing?"

"You should be paralyzed with fear, not escaping."

"Get back here!"

The heads screamed out at us, causing Chess to tense in my arms, but I ignored them. Let them bitch and moan. My eyes were all for the mirror, and I wasn't stopping for anyone or anything.

Just as I reached the mirror, one of them asked, "What are you?"

This time answered but didn't stop as a confident smile spread over my face. "The one who will save us all, even your sorry asses." With those parting words, I shoved Chess and me through the tar-like substance and we fell out the other side. We landed at the feet of a waiting Alice.

CHAPTER 11

CAN WE KEEP HIM?

ALICE WAS STANDING in the middle of the queen's room, her hands on her hips and an impatient frown on her face. There were no guards in sight, and my mother was mysteriously gone as well.

"Where is everybody?" I set Chess on the ground, but he stayed latched onto my pant leg, his gaze unwavering as he took in Alice's form.

"I was in the library with the guards where we were having a good old time playing guess which guard was real. Come to find out that guards aren't very talented in seeing through a glamour." She smiled at the memory, and then frowned, and shrugged. "Then a servant came running in, screaming about some monster bird at the palace gates. They went rushing out, not paying me any mind. So I came up here. Your mother wasn't in here, but who could blame her, look at this décor." She glanced around the room and made a face.

"Oh." What else was I supposed to say? Lucky us, a disaster had come just in the nick of time? Though, more than likely it was our fault there was an emergency in the first place. A monster bird? Sounded like the JubJub to me.

"Who's that?" Alice pointed down to the child fastened to my leg and then her face brightened. "Oh my goodness. That's not, is it?"

I nodded my head and bent down to pry Chess off me. "Yep. We seem to have a situation on our hands."

"But he's so cute!" she squealed, clapping her hands together before kneeling on the floor next to us.

Chess stared at her for a moment, and then gave me a questioning look over his shoulder. I made a motion with my hand, urging him forward. That seemed to be all he needed before he ran into Alice's open arms. What do you know? He was a ladies man even at this age.

I watched as Alice cooed and cuddled with the feline, a small smile on my face. He was just too adorable, and he had such innocence to him. It was tempting to keep him this way forever. But I couldn't. I hadn't been lying when I told my mother that I needed him, I did. Not just because I felt I was guilty he got taken because of me, but he really was the only chance we had if something happened to me. I couldn't go up against the Shadows without a backup plan, and he was it.

"Not that he isn't the cutest thing I have ever seen," Alice started, holding Chess in her lap, "But how did this happen?"

I sighed, running a hand through my hair. "From what I understand when the Bandersnatch feeds off your fear they reduce you backwards in time. This," I gestured toward the feline, "Is all that was left of him when I got there."

"Oh you poor thing!" Alice cried out, pulling him tightly against her chest. "How horrible it must have been for you and to torture a child?" she shook her head in disgust.

"Yes, we have already established that, any ideas how to change him back?"

"Change me back?" Chess poked his head up from Alice's embrace. "To what?"

The question was so endearing; I seriously had to force myself not to start baby talking to him. I could tell by the look on Alice's face that she was having the same issue.

"Do we have to change him back? I mean, can't we just leave him the way he is? Then he can have another chance at a good childhood!" Her eyes lit up and she glanced down at Chess with a smile. "Would you like that, little one? Do you want to come home with Mama Alice?"

Before Chess could answer, I jumped in, "No. Absolutely not."

"Why not?" she pouted, giving me her best puppy dog eyes. "It would be so fun."

"Fun?" I gaped. "Not only is it wrong, but where are you planning on raising him? At my house? I don't think so." I shook my head at her.

"Don't you want to give him the childhood he never had? Then maybe he wouldn't have grown up to become such a rake." She petted a hand down his dirty pink hair, her face softening with her words.

It wasn't like I didn't want Chess to have better memories. God knew he needed them. But I couldn't imagine having him living in my home the way he was now. It wasn't just wrong. It was creepy.

Every time I saw him I would remember what he used to look like and then how we almost were together. Also, what was I going to do once he grew up? I didn't want to see him go through puberty and start dating girls. It was hard enough even thinking about him after what happened between us. No. There was no way it would work. We had to change him back.

"We can't, Alice. We need him at full strength. And while this age might seem appealing." I held my hand out to him, my heart leapt when he jumped from Alice's arms to take my hand. "It wouldn't be right of us to just leave him this way without his say in it. And, you don't even know who we are do you, little guy?" In a moment of weakness, I rubbed my nose against his causing him to giggle.

"Why doesn't he remember anything?" Alice approached us, her face sobering.

"I'm assuming it is because he's a child again, and at this age, he didn't know either of us." I shrugged and then turned my attention back to the child in my arms. "By the way, I'm Kat and this is Alice."

Chess peered up at us through lowered lashes, suddenly seeming shy as he muttered.

"What?" I arched my ear down to him.

"I said it's nice to meet you!" he shouted it out, and then covered his mouth, his face turning beet red. "Opps."

"It's all right. It's nice to meet you too... again." I ended awkwardly and then looked to Alice. "So, any ideas?"

Alice thought about it for a moment, placing a hand on her face as she looked up to the ceiling. "Well...why don't you ask Seer? She usually seems to know what is going on. Maybe she can help?"

"But she's all the way in the UnSeelie Court. I really don't want to drag a child through all that." I clutched him to me as if to protect him from the horrors of the Underground.

"Why don't you use that compact that Pat gave you?" she pointed down to my jeans pocket where I had stored the mirror. "Maybe you can speak to her through it?"

I had forgotten about the mirror Pat had given me in his shop. It was supposed to be used in case of an emergency and looking at the child in my arms, I constituted this as a major emergency. Just hopefully it hadn't gotten broken through all the scuffles we'd been through.

Setting Chess down on the ground, I dug into my pocket until my hand touched the cool metal of the compact and drew it out. Holding it in my hand, I flipped open the cover. I let out the breath I had been holding when I saw the mirror was still intact. Finally some luck!

"Okay, so how do I use it?" I turned it over in my hand, looking for an on switch or some kind of glyphs like there were on the rest of the mirrors in the Underground.

While looking, my finger brushed the surface of the mirror, and a slight ripple of power sent a shock of magic through my hand. Jumping in place, I stared down at the mirror. The reflection had turned into mercury like substance. I thought of Seer, of where she might be. The last place I had seen her was at the door to the Seelie Court, but I doubted she was still there. More than likely she was in the Mushroom City, lounging on one of her beds of fungi with her pipe in her hand. At my thoughts, the mirror swirled about in the compact, its silver like surface morphed into a scene that seemed more like a traveling circus than Seer's home.

Opalaughts ran across the grass, some the size of Trip and some smaller, I assumed the smaller were children. There were brownies there as well, but the only reason I knew that was because they had the same brown shade of skin as Mop, each with matching black eyes and hair. Among those I recognized were creatures I'd never seen before. Lions with snake tails and wings, what could have very well been a real life unicorn, and then there were...the satyrs.

A shiver ran through me at the sight of the half-goat half-human creatures. While I was happy to see that Romp and Piper were nowhere in sight, just the presence of a satyr caused my stomach to roll. I had not had good experiences with satyrs and had no reason to believe that any of them would be different than the rapist bastards I'd encountered before.

The one creature in the midst of all the Fae that I couldn't see was Seer. I moved the mirror around the room in my hand, trying to see around the corners of the frame, but it was a useless effort. I could only see as far as the mirror allowed.

"Um...excuse me." The moment my words came out of my mouth and reached their ears everyone froze. Their heads turned in my direction in slow motion. They blinked their eyes at me before there was a sudden exclamation from the horde, and they ran toward the mirror, all of them talking at once, moving their hands adamantly while trying to explain something to me. What, I hadn't the faintest.

"Hold on, hold on." I held my hand up, pulling the mirror back from my face so they could see me better. "One at a time. I can't understand what you are saying."

They quieted and one of the brownies, a little woman with a blue dress that matched a hat on top of her head stepped forward. She had bangles on her arms and a thin line of hair along her chin. While she had facial hair, there was no doubt she was female due to the long lashes that surrounded her eyes and rosy lips that she spoke out of.

"Lady, we are so happy to see you." Her voice was so low and sultry that would rival even one of the High Fae of the Seelie Court.

"I can tell." I couldn't help but smile at them before frowning. "What's going on? Why are there so many of you at Seer's? And where is Seer?"

"You do not know?" the shock on her face matched those around her. The brownie looked among the other faces as if she thought she had heard me wrong.

"Know what?"

"We have come together to face the darkness as one. When you face the Shadows, we shall be at your disposal should you need us." She nodded her head along with those around her.

"That's great and all, and I appreciate the gesture, but I'm not sure there is really anything you can do to help. It's kind of a solo thing." I grimaced at the way that came out. I didn't want to sound full of myself, I would take any help I could get. But the spell had to be said by me, and the blood mine. No one else could help me with that.

"We know that." She snapped; her eyes filled with annoyance. "But we can lend you our magic in your time of need. After all, it is you who are saving us."

The grouch in her voice reminded me of a certain brownie that was blatantly missing and I had an idea. "You wouldn't happen to be Mop's wife, would you?"

A brilliant smile covered her face. "Why, yes, I am."

I opened my mouth to ask where Mop was when Alice shoved me aside to look in the mirror. "While this is all very interesting, we are looking for Seer."

"What are you doing?" I whispered, turning my head toward her.

Keeping her voice low as well, she shot me an impatient frown. "We might have lost the queen and her guards for now but they might be back any minute. We don't have time for pleasantries."

She was right. We had a brief reprieve for now, but who knew when my mother would come back, and when she did, if she would even let us leave? Thinking about that, I didn't think staying here in her bedroom was a good idea anymore.

"Hold on a moment." I held my finger up to the mirror and turned to Alice. "You're right, we can't stay here anymore. Not even to fix Chess." I gestured down to the boy waiting patiently on the floor next to us, his face enthralled by our conversation.

"Then what should we do?" Alice asked.

"You should come here." Our eyes locked back onto the compact where Mop's wife was still talking. "Then you can find the Seer yourself and get all the answers you need."

Sounded like a good idea to me. The only problem was getting there. The mirror to the Bandersnatch was the only mirror I had seen in the whole room, and I hadn't really been paying much attention to where we were going on our way here. I had no idea if there were any mirrors close by that could be used to go to the UnSeelie Court.

Turning to Alice, I asked, "Any idea how to get out of here?"

"Oh, plenty," she answered. "But we'll have to hurry. All the mirrors I saw were wide out in the open, and I have no clue how to tell which one would take us where we want to go." She fluffed her skirt around her and seemed to think on it.

Pulling my attention back to the mirror, I said, "We'll figure it out. Just tell Seer we are coming. We have a little..." My gaze fell on the top of Chess' small head. "...problem we need her assistance with."

"No worries. I will deliver the message verbatim. Just get yourselves here and safe." She gave a short downward jerk of her head and then the mirror went blank.

I tucked the mirror into my pocket and then held my arms out to Chess. "Come on, little one, we've got to get going."

Not even hesitating, he climbed into my arms. Giving Alice a look that asked if she was ready, we moved to the door. I turned the knob, and slowly creaked the door open. My eyes peeked into the hallway.

"Do you see anyone?" Alice asked behind me as Chess' small voice asked, "Where are we going?"

"No, I don't." I answered and then to Chess, "We are going to make you big again, and to do that we have to get some help."

"Big again? But I'm already big!" he held his arms out to show me just how big he was. Smiling at him, I rubbed my nose against his once more, getting me a giggle in response before I pushed the door the rest of the way open and stepped out into the hallway.

Turning to Alice, I gestured for her to lead. "After you."

Following me into the hall, she looked both ways, her face creased in concentration. After a moment, she pointed a hand down the right side. "I believe the mirror I saw is this way."

Letting her take the lead, we hurried down the hallway; the only sound was our feet hitting the marble floor. My arms began to ache from holding Chess but putting him down wasn't an option. We needed speed and from prior experience, children were slow and easily distracted. I was lucky he had cooperated so easily so far.

Alice came to an abrupt stop that caused me to trip over my own feet and almost made me drop Chess in the process. Shooting her a glare, I wasted no time going to the mirrors frame. Reaching my hand up to activate it, Chess' voice stopped me.

"Can I do it?" his large green eyes were intently focused on the glyphs along the mirrors frame. His eyes sparkled with an eagerness I had only seen in his older self's eyes.

"Sure you can." I grabbed his hand in mine and led it up to the frame. When he was close enough to it, I let him go, watching to see if he would know what to do.

I shouldn't have worried; he slid his hand along the frame as if he had done it a hundred times before. The frame lit up and the surface swelled activating the portal.

"Good job." I gave him a little squeeze and then exchanged a look with Alice, who nodded in response.

I didn't know where this mirror went but anywhere was better than in the middle of the Seelie Palace. What was that saying again? Beggars can't be choosers? Well in this moment, I was a beggar, but I still didn't want to end up ass deep in more trouble than we were already in. I was running out of patience. When that happened I got stupid, and when I got stupid, that meant things were going to get messy and fast.

CHAPTER 12

UNSEELIE COURT

IT WAS ASKING too much to come out anywhere near the Seer's home. Tall green hedges surrounded us as we stepped out of the mirror and onto the greyish cobblestone of the UnSeelie Queen's garden.

Mab, the UnSeelie Queen and my ex-fiancé's mother, was not how many people would portray her. In stories she was the evil queen who would crush your heart in a moment of boredom. When in reality, she was just an over passionate woman who loved her son dearly. Seeing as I broke her son's heart, and was the reason he had been taken from her, I was probably the last person she wanted to see.

I sat Chess on the ground and took his small hand in mine. I had only been here once before, and I didn't know if there were flesh eating plants who'd love to take a chunk out of a cute kid like him. Not that he was in any hurry to go it on his own.

He clung to my hand like I would disappear at any moment. His eyes were round and so full of fear that it made me hurt inside. From what I'd heard from Chess, this hadn't been a good age for him, and I couldn't imagine what he had already experienced at such a tender age. The Bandersnatch probably hadn't helped any either.

"Where are we?" Alice asked, stepping out of the mirror, her head swiveling around.

"No place good." I took a cautious step forward, bringing Chess with me to peer around one of the hedges. The last time I had been here there had been singing, but the lack of singing this time didn't make me any less wary of running into the queen.

From where we stood it seemed like we had come into the garden from the opposite side than last time. The fountain with the statue of a tree and three people, a man and two women, was on the opposite side of the clearing. This side of the clearing had small shrubs lining the outside. On the inside I could see where I had met Mab once before, when I thought I was just a human with Fae ancestors, and not the Seelie Princess.

I waved at Alice over my shoulder as I directed Chess into the garden. "Come on."

I sort of tip toed down the stone path, my eyes darting left and right. It wouldn't help to be caught unaware in somewhere I was in no way supposed to be. Why they even had a mirror near the garden was strange. Did she make unexpected calls? And if so, why would she do it out in the open where anyone could hear her?

"I don't like this," Alice whispered behind me. I couldn't disagree. It was too quiet. Usually, there were birds or some kind of background noise, but even the fountain wasn't running. Where was everyone?

"Me either. Let's just get out of here." We came around the bushes and entered the main part of the garden. From here I could see where I had met up with Mab before, but what I saw there made me stop in place.

The roses. The white roses that Dorian had planted for me when we got engaged that had later bled red, were dying. The vibrant color of the petals was brown and sagging. The branches and leaves were black as if someone had taken a lighter to them.

"Pitiful, isn't it?"

My spine stiffened at the sound of the UnSeelie Queen's voice. Dark and sensual with a slightly sharp edge to it. She had always had a great phone sex voice. But hearing it now just made my skin crawl.

"What happened?" I didn't turn away from the roses, but I did draw Chess in front of me so he wasn't in her line of sight.

"You don't know?" I could sense her presence as she soundlessly made her way across the garden. She stopped beside us, her black dress brushing against my legs. Just that simple touch made me want to run away from her screaming. She hadn't offered violence, yet, but the thick tension in the air said that it was only a matter of time before it came up.

"Why would I?" I shifted my weight until I was turned toward her.

Like my mother, she had a sense of style that had become expected of her. Dark dresses that clung to her figure but also billowed out around her like a spider web seeking its meal. Where my mother was light and cold, Mab was the night and all that came with it. She offered passion and darkness, a place to be you without judgment. The Seelie Court was supposed to be about honesty and chivalry, but my mother had corrupted what it really meant to be the Seelie Queen. I could only hope one day they would be put back on the right path, even if I wasn't there to see it.

"You seem to know so much already, I would expect the savior to know when she was destroying one's life." She said the words like she was complimenting me on my hair.

"I didn't mean for this to happen. I didn't force him to join the Shadows because I broke up with him. He did that all on his own." I took a half step toward her but stopped and sighed. I didn't owe her an explanation, and she wouldn't accept it even if I gave her one.

"It wasn't my fault. I didn't know what would happen," she mimicked my words back to me an edge of anger coloring her voice. "It seems to me, dear, that you never take any of the blame on yourself and expect others to just deal with it."

I opened my mouth to protest but closed it. Arguing was going to get me nowhere. She was determined to hate me, and there was nothing I could say or do short of turning back time that would change it.

Instead, I turned away from her without a word, pushing Chess in front of me.

"Leaving so soon?" Her voice called out to me, I ignored it and kept walking until she said, "But what of our dear Cheshire, do you not wish to return him to his true form?"

Stopping once more, I took in a deep breath before exhaling as I turned back. "And what would you know of it?"

The smile that tipped her lips was one that said she knew she had something we wanted, but we weren't going to get it from her without paying for it first. It also meant that if I wanted her help nothing short of begging would suffice. And I didn't beg. Not for anyone or anything.

When she didn't answer immediately, I half spun on my heel before her voice stopped me again, "What would you give to save him?"

"What do you mean?" Suspicion began to creep into my mind.

"I mean exactly what I said. What would you give?" She moved across the cobblestone as if floating, a trait she had passed down to her son no doubt. Her dress moved around her like an extension of herself, gliding and shifting as if it were a breathing, living, being.

Mab stopped a mere foot away, causing Alice, who had had the good sense to keep quiet, to shift until she was behind me. I pressed Chess closer to me until he let go of my hand and took his place wrapped around my leg, his tail playing along the side of my jeans.

"Almost anything." I wasn't an all or nothing kind of girl, there were just some things you couldn't give and saying anything might have opened me up to all kinds of sadistic things I couldn't even think of.

"Almost anything?" her brows rose in surprise. "I would think you would give anything for the creature who stole your love from my son." Her eyes zeroed in on Chess, and the look wasn't kind.

"Chess didn't steal anything, I gave it freely. Your son couldn't accept me for what I am," I stated between clenched teeth.

"And what are you? Fae? Human? Savior? You aren't exactly one or the other, are you?" her voice was condescending and full of exasperation. "It seems you are somehow stuck in the middle of something you have no right to be in. The role you play isn't even yours, is it?" This time her eyes and voice were all for Chess, sending some kind of secret message that I couldn't decipher.

"Enough of your games, do you know how to fix Chess or not?" I growled, drawing her attention back to me.

"It's not a matter of fixing him." Her long, blood red nails reached down to Chess, who cringed from her touch and clung to me tighter.

"Then what is it?" Alice spoke up from behind me, causing Mab's gaze to harden.

"Do not speak to me, pretender!" she hissed her words, her face contorting into a menacing snarl, and for a moment, I thought she might lash out at her before her face calmed and she returned to her normal cool self. She glanced down at Chess once more, this time, the smile on her face was more curious than evil. "The Bandersnatch is not a forgiving creature."

"So we've noticed." My lips twisted into a frown.

"What they took was not just sin but magic. Dreams." Her eyes lit up with a hunger I had only seen on a few Faes' faces, and none of those meetings had ended well.

"Okay," I drew out, my patience growing thin. "Then how do we make him, you know, big again? Put the magic back?"

"Exactly." She knelt on the ground, her skirts smoothing underneath her on their own. Mab reached out but did not touch Chess, her hand sort of just hovered an inch away from his face. "Much magic has been removed, and it will take just as much to put it back."

"But how do we put it back? We can't just go back to the Bandersnatch and ask 'could you kindly give Chess' magic back, please?' Might as well ask them to destroy the Shadows while we are at it." I snorted, placing a hand on one hip and cocking it to the side.

"Do not get smart with me, child." Mab stood abruptly, getting so close to my face, I dropped my arm and stepped back. "You have been lucky so far to have found help when needed, but one day your luck will run out." She snapped her fingers in front of my face with a growl. "And all that you once held dear will be snuffed out, and there will be nothing you can do to stop it."

I had a feeling we weren't talking about me anymore, and it made me pity her. She had not lost her son once but twice in a short amount of time. Well, short in Fae years. And the person responsible for her misery was standing right in front of her, and she couldn't do anything to avenge her son in fear of the Shadows destroying everything. It was a sad day when your only hope was also the one you despised above all others.

"I'm sorry," I murmured, apologizing for more than just my attitude. "Please continue."

Her face became living marble, her eyes the only thing showing life as she began to speak, "As it so happens, you are correct. You cannot request the magic be returned but you can replace it." I opened my mouth to ask how but she beat me to it, "With someone else's magic."

Someone else's magic? I placed a hand on top of Chess' head, smoothing the hair between his ears as they twitched at my touch. "How?"

At that one word it was like a light switch had been thrown and her face was alive once more. A smile spread across her face so wide that I feared it would rip her head in half. The Joker had nothing on this woman.

When her hand reached up and cupped my cheek in her hand, I forced myself not to flinch, not to cower back. She leaned in close until our lips were only a hairs breath away from each other. I almost thought she would kiss me but instead, she said, "By giving yours up in return."

I jerked back from her, and my feet stumbled beneath me, causing Chess to release me or be thrown to the ground. Thankfully, he chose the former and it was only me that landed on my backside glaring up at a smirking Mab.

"I can't just give up my magic to save him." I shook my head, sadness filling my face. "Not if I'm to save everyone else."

Mab gave an elegant shrug. "You do not have to give up all of your magic. Just enough to return him to his rightful size, but..." her words trailed off, her eyes sliding away to the side.

"But what?" I crawled to my knees, my hands stinging where they had skidded against the stone.

"The exchange of one's magic is a serious thing. It cannot be taken lightly, and those who do it will be bound forever. Your heart will be linked to his, your magic as one. If one of you dies the other will feel it for the rest of their life. Like a wound that will never heal. Could you handle that?"

Could I? I loved him, yes, but could I give up a part of myself to someone who might or might not love me in return? I gulped and met Chess' sparkling green eyes that were so full of innocence and fear. I couldn't leave him like this. Not if I could help him.

"Yes," I gasped out, my heart in my throat, "I can."

"Wonderful." She clapped her hands together, her nails clicking as they touched. "Now, as you may recall, on your first trip to the Underground..." she gestured to me in disdain. "You had the misfortune to ingest too much faerie wine."

"I remember, and your son did something to draw it out." I felt my face heat as I remembered. I had been so nervous on my first trip to the Seelie Court and Gab had been asking so many personal questions I had gotten a little carried away with the drink they were serving. I didn't know it was faerie wine, or what it could do to a human, but Dorian knew.

When Dorian found me I was ready to run off with Bastian and blow my cover. Instead, I found myself out on the balcony thinking I was about to get kissed when in reality he drew the faerie magic out of me and into himself. I remembered the sparkling blue as it floated out of my mouth and into his.

"Yes, he did." She nodded her head, the first sign of approval showing since I had appeared. "You will do something similar to our dear Moderator but in reverse."

"How do I do that?" I watched Chess as I asked my question, giving him a weak smile so he wouldn't be afraid.

"Just will it to be so and it will be." She waved her hand in an elaborate circle as if her words answered everything.

Frowning at her explanation, I crawled over to Chess on my knees. He watched my movements with adoration in his eyes. He trusted me so explicitly it made my insides ache. In a few short moments, the only emotion he would feel for me would be indifference.

"What's going on?" his small voice asked as I placed my hands on the sides of his face.

I shushed him, bringing my forehead to lean against his. "Don't worry, I won't let anything bad happen to you. We are just going to make you all better again."

"Will it hurt?"

Shaking my head, I smiled gently. "No, not at all. Can you close your eyes for me?" I leaned back away from him as he nodded and closed his eyes.

I placed my thumbs on his jaw and pressed down, urging him to open his mouth. My magic swirled and burned inside me as I drew it to life. I had never done something like this before. Growing plant life and animating vegetables was one thing, but passing my magic to someone else without the intention of hurting them? I just hoped I didn't kill us both.

The magic sizzled and fizzed as it crawled out of my stomach and up my throat. I forced myself not to swallow as it tickled my larynx. As it built up in my mouth, I opened my lips, pressing my mouth close to his. The magic left me as easy as breathing, and as I took another breath and let it out, more passed from me to him.

I couldn't tell the affects right away, but the more energy that passed from my lips and into his, the older his face became, and the more light-headed I felt. The baby fat to his face shrunk, turning into a more defined jawline and cheekbones. His chest and shoulders expanded, the rest of his body following, causing me to arch up to reach his face from my place on the ground.

I knew the moment he was himself again. I felt it in my heart. Like a light switch had been flipped and everything in the world made sense again. His eyes flipped open, his emerald eyes wide with shock and horror. At me or at himself I wasn't sure, and at that moment, it took all I had to keep my hands on his face, and even that was failing.

Eventually, it was Chess who stopped me. He pulled my hands from him, closing his mouth so I couldn't breathe any more magic into him, and drew me to his chest as I had done in the Bandersnatch.

"Oh, kitten. What have you done?" he asked. I gave him a weak smile before my eyels fluttered closed, and there was nothing but the sound of his heart beating in time with mine.

CHAPTER 13
OF ONE HEART

WHEN I AWOKE I was no longer in Mab's garden but staring up at a wooden roof. Every inch of me screamed, from the balls of my feet to the hairs on top of my head. Even breathing hurt.

What the hell happened? Chess. I was giving some of my magic to Chess and then I passed out. God, I felt horrible. I so was not doing that ever again.

I lifted a hand to my head as I inched up from whoever's bed I was laying in. Each movement was like tiny needles were being shoved into my nerve endings. This wasn't like being hung over from using too much power, this was like I got hit by a Mac truck and had been in a coma for the last six months. The kind of pain that made you just want to curl into a ball and die.

I tried to ignore the pain and figure out where exactly I was, and where the hell everyone else was? Achingly slow, I turned my head from the ceiling to take in the small bedroom I was currently residing in. The bed was only big enough to fit two people comfortably. The comforter that had been thrown over me was patched in multicolored cloth. The rest of the room wasn't much different.

A nightstand made of the same kind of wood as the ceiling sat next to the bed; it wasn't the usual shape you would expect to see a nightstand. It curved and twisted like it couldn't decide what shape to take. The three-drawer dresser on the other side of the small room wasn't any different. How they got their clothes in there was beyond me.

There was only one door that was left ajar, letting in low voices that I couldn't decipher. I tried to move into a sitting position once more and cried out at the effort. My pained cry must have been heard from the other room, because the voices halted and a rush of footsteps came my way.

The half open door was thrown open and in the doorway stood Chess. He was no longer a child and the rags he had been wearing had been replaced with a pale lavender tunic that laced at the neck. His pants were a darker shade lavender and looked like they were made of some kind of felt. To top it all off, they were tucked into knee-high boots that blended in with the fabric.

The moment I saw him my breathing became easier, and my pain didn't matter as much anymore. Was this what Mab had meant? Would we have to be around each other to ever feel normal? If so, it would make using the bathroom a very interesting venture.

"How are you feeling, pet?" Chess knelt by the bed, Alice and Hatter bringing up the rear; worry etching all of their faces.

The décor finally made sense. We were in Hatter's house. Though, how we got here was still a mystery.

I had only met Hatter once, at the Seelie Court. There he had been a sore thumb sticking out in the midst of a room of golden hornets. Here in his own home, he seemed more relaxed and less likely to throw up at any moment.

His head was noticeably bare, no doubt because we were inside. His silver hair was pulled back in a loose ponytail that trailed over his shoulder and brushed the base of his multicolored vest that lay on top of a magenta dress shirt. His pants were a dark emerald green and his shoes a bicolored red and blue. Overall, he should have looked ridiculous, but he didn't, and by the way Alice was sneaking glances at him she didn't think so either.

Turning my attention back to Chess, I tried to speak and then coughed at the dryness in my throat. Alice produced a cup from somewhere and handed it to Chess who in turn held it up to my lips. Usually, I would have made some kind of smart remark about not being a child but my arms still felt like they weighed a hundred pounds.

Thankfully, only water was in the cup, but part of me wouldn't have refused something stronger. Not Hatter's tea strong, but a shot of vodka wouldn't have been unwelcome.

All eyes focused on me as I finished my drink and cleared my throat. "What happened?" My words came out in a sort of croak that sounded like I smoked ten packs a day.

"You fainted, of course," Alice answered. "You know, if you keep this up they are going to start calling you the fainter rather than the savior." I glared at her but from the twinkle in her eye could tell she was just kidding. Not that she was wrong. I seemed to be doing quite a lot of fainting nowadays. Chalk it up to the unusually high amount of magic I was emitting lately.

A shock ran up my arm, jerking my attention from Alice to my hand where Chess had placed his on top of mine. That was interesting. It was like a sort of buzzing along the underside of my skin. Not exactly an unpleasant feeling but different to be sure.

My eyes rose from our joined hands to meet his. Unlike Alice, who seemed to be trying to make light of the situation, which was usually Chess' job, his eyes were full of worry, but also underneath it was a need. The same need that was beginning to build in me.

"I'm fine," I finally said, causing some of his worry to fall away, but the hunger was still there and with Alice and Hatter in the room it was making me uncomfortable.

Hatter, who up until this point had been a silent observer, made an awkward noise in his throat. "Alice dear, let's give them some privacy."

Alice let Hatter lead her out of the room, and the moment the door clicked shut, Chess' mouth was on mine. Still partly in pain, I made a small sound in the back of my throat but didn't push him away. It was like coming home: the feel of his upper body pressed against mine, his lips moving across my own, and the taste of him as he caressed my tongue. It hadn't been like this before. The overwhelming need to be as close to him as possible, to crawl inside of him if I could.

I had always been attracted to Chess. From the moment he unwrapped himself from his vine-covered throne, a part of me wanted him. It took a while for me to finally admit that I wanted him more than just physically, and when we finally came together, it had been explosive and wonderful. Until that is, it wasn't. That thought, had me pushing him away even though my very being screamed at me for it.

"Wait. Stop," I said between closed mouth kisses, my hands still twisting in the fabric of his shirt. His response was to trail his mouth down the side of my neck, a low growl rumbling from his chest. The sound shot straight between my thighs.

My insides melted as his mouth found that spot between my neck and shoulder that made me groan. He climbed up on the bed and pressed me back down onto the mattress. With the cover between us, we couldn't get the friction we needed. There needed to be more touching, more skin.

"What's wrong with us?" Chess' voice against the side of my neck caused a shiver to run through me and was just enough to give me the strength to push him away and slip out of the bed.

I kept my back to him, because the sight of him on the bed rumpled and ready would make me want to dive back in. I felt my face heat at my lack of self-control. I was pretty sure I knew the answer to his question, but I had never thought it would cause such a reaction.

"The queen warned me something like this would happen." I cleared my throat, trying to sound more normal and not so wanton. "Well, not this exactly, but she said we would be more connected."

"I don't understand." I heard him move from the bed, and I tensed as his body stood just behind me. Not touching, just there. "Why would you save me?" I felt his hands reach up and almost touch my arms before he dropped them again.

"I couldn't just leave you like that."

"But you could have. After the way I treated you, I didn't deserve anything less." His voice was low and broken as if he thought he really deserved being put in the Bandersnatch.

"No, you didn't." I shook my head, not turning to look at him for fear of what I would do. "If I punished every guy who'd ever been an asshole to me there'd be no men left." I gave a small laugh but my heart wasn't in it.

"Kat." This time when his hands reached up they did touch me, and the feel of his skin against mine, just his hands pressed against my arms, almost blew my hard won control.

"Don't." My voice broke with that one word and my eyes burned. I wouldn't cry damn it. How can my body and soul crave his touch and my heart break at the same time? It wasn't fair.

"Kitten."

I shrugged, causing his hands to fall off my arms. Turning around with a laugh, I gave him a sad smile. "You can't help who you love and who you don't." I took a deep breath, dragging myself away from him while mentally building a wall between us.

"So, what it seems like to me is that the exchange of magic has a bit more to it than what I'd thought." I stared at the nightstand pretending like he wasn't in the room at all. "The side effects are more intense, not only making us want to be near each other, but the need to touch one another is almost overwhelming. The only way I see this working without both of us going insane is to just go about our lives as normal, I mean after the Shadows are beaten. You can go back to doing whatever you did before, and we can just pretend like this never happened and hope the affects fade after time." Even as I said the words, I hated it. I didn't want to pretend we never happened, but I couldn't pretend like I didn't love him or watch as he paraded around with more of his playthings.

"Do you really think that will work?" my gaze jerked away from the nightstand at the anger in his voice. "While you were out, it was killing me not to be by your side while you slept. Hatter had to give me some tea just so I would stop running a hole in his floor." He took a step toward me, his tail whipping behind him in a rigid path. "We are like two sides of a magnet. We are drawn to each other and no amount of lying to ourselves will stop that."

The feral look he gave me made things clench so tightly below that I gasped. His smell, his presence, all of it was like I was a drug addict and my drug of choice was zeroing in on me, leaving me with no place to go.

"I can't do this," I muttered more to myself than Chess, who had stopped in front of me. "Please."

His hands reached up to stroke the sides of my face while his tail wrapped around my leg pulling me into him. The moment my hands touched his again, I knew I was lost. His mouth ghosted across my forehead, creating a path down my face and across each cheek. My eyes fluttered shut as his lips brushed across my eyelids. When he finally reached my mouth, my resolve had weakened so completely that I wasn't strong enough to tell myself, no, to tell him to stop, but I was strong enough to find out exactly what I was getting into.

"This is just sex, right? Just sex." It was more of a reassurance to me than a question, but it was Chess' response that undid me.

"It will never be just sex, Kat." My chest warmed at the surety of his words and the analytical side of me wanted to know exactly what he meant, but in that moment, he picked me up by the back of my legs and pressed our bodies together. All thoughts were lost and the only thing that mattered was him.

My legs wrapped around his waist and my mouth sought out his until we were melded together as close as possible with our clothing still on. I slipped my tongue between his lips, sliding it back and forth between his sharpened canines.

There was a certain way you had to kiss someone who had fangs; otherwise you would cut the crap out of your tongue every time you kissed. My mind might be clouded with lust, my body overtaken by the magic that drew us to each other, but I wasn't so far gone that I couldn't remember not to slice myself up. Chess, on the other hand, didn't seem to care about getting hurt. He attacked my mouth like he was searching for the Holy Grail and the only place he would find it would be in the back of my throat.

Trying to move things along, I pulled on his shirt until he let go of my mouth long enough to bring me over to the bed. My back hit the mattress, and I had a brief moment where I wondered if Alice and Hatter had done it on here before Chess was back before me sans any clothes. My mind didn't have a chance to comprehend the gorgeous sight of a naked Chess before he was pulling at my clothing.

My clothing came off and then it was a sort of blur. Skin pressed against skin, leaving a trail of heat with every touch. Then he was inside me, stretching me, filling me, and a sense of absolute completion overcame me. My gaze locked onto his and I knew I wasn't the only one feeling it.

Growls and moans built up as we moved together, so loud that if I had been in my right mind it would have made me worried about Hatter and Alice hearing. But the more we touched each other, the more my magic seemed to come alive, and the glow that had shown up the last time we had been together was almost blinding as we reached our peak.

Afterward, when we had come back down and we separated the urge to be with him wasn't so intense. I had time to think about what we had done and what it meant. Panic rose in me. My pulse thudded so hard beneath the surface that it hurt, and I was about to bolt, but Chess' arm wrapped around me.

"I can taste your fear, like a heavy bitter tang on my tongue." His clawed hand stroked my arm in a soothing motion. He let a purr vibrate out of his chest and all the tension in me seemed to relax. "Better?"

"Yes." I turned slightly to him until I could see his eyes. A languid, satisfied expression covered his face and I hated to destroy it with what I had to say. "It feels different now, doesn't it? Like I still want to be near you, but I don't feel like I'm going to die if I don't."

He leaned up onto his elbow and his hand brushed through my hair along the side of my face, a small smile on his lips. "I know what you mean. Maybe it will always be this way?"

"Like what?" I pulled back until his hand dropped away. "We stay away from each other for as long as possible until the need to be near each other builds up again, then we fuck like bunnies before going back to our normal lives?"

His lips curled down and he sighed. The sound of it was irritated even to me. "No, Katherine, we will not just fuck and then go away." His hand grasped the side of my hip and pulled me to him in almost a violent motion. I put my hands up to keep us from being flush against each other. I needed some distance, even though the pull between us had lessened.

"Then what do you suggest?" Heat bubbled in my stomach and it had nothing to do with sex and everything to do with rage.

"You weren't even listening before, were you?" his anger answered mine but his held such a ferocity that it made my palms sweat and my pulse race. "Must I spell it out for your delicate human ears for you to understand that I love you?"

I blinked. Once. Twice. Three times before I shook my head and asked, "You love me?"

His anger seemed to dissipate at my question and his expression softened. "Yes, silly girl. I do."

"Then why did you..." I started.

"Say what I did?"

"Yeah." I nodded, my eyes going down to stare at his chest. I didn't have the courage to look him in the eyes as he answered.

"The prince."

"What about him?" I frowned harder but my gaze finally rose to meet his. "You're not afraid of him, are you?"

"Not of him per say, but what he might do to you. On his own our dark prince can be as vicious and as unforgiving as the Bandersnatch, but when he had the chance to get the love of his life back, he had mellowed out some. If I had pronounced anything other than friendship with you, making him believe he didn't have a chance anymore, there was no telling what he would do."

"You mean like join the Shadows?"

"Exactly." He tapped my nose with his finger and I wrinkled it at the touch. "But dear Alice has brought me up to speed, and it seems like my charade was all for not." He sat up in the bed with a distraught sigh.

I grabbed his arm and pressed my naked flesh against him. "It wasn't for nothing, we're together now. So, no more secrets, right?" My hand slid beneath the covers and played along the inside of his thigh.

Chess took me in his arms with a playful grin. "No more secrets."

He captured my mouth in his as he eased us back down to the bed. Desire curled in me as he slithered between my thighs and brought my legs up around his waist. But before he could slide home, a knock on the door followed by Hatter's voice interrupted us, "If you two are quite finished, I would like my bedroom back now."

CHAPTER 14

SEARCHING

MY FACE COULDN'T get any redder as I stood before Hatter and Alice with Chess at my side. If he was fazed it didn't show, but the knowing smile on Alice's face was unsettling, and I knew I would be hearing it from her for weeks to come.

"Now that we are all here, back on our feet, and back to the right size." Alice gave me a sly grin before continuing, "We need to discuss what we are going to do next. Hatter here has kindly offered us his home as a base of operations." She clasped hands with the serious Fae, and they exchanged a look that made me wonder what they had been doing while Chess and I were busy. We would definitely be having a talk before all this was over. If I was still here that is.

"Well, we need to find the Shadows for one," Chess said, his tail wrapping around my leg. The urge to touch each other was still there and having that small connection was enough to calm it.

I shook my head at him, my want to be near him not overshadowing my own good sense. "There is no point in finding them if we don't know the ritual to get rid of them. And we left my mother's before we had a chance to ask her."

"We had a good reason, though," Alice argued, gracing Chess with a pointed look. "We couldn't have asked her while Cheshire was in such a vulnerable state. Who knows what the queen might have asked for in return?"

"She won't be getting anything in return." I shifted my weight to one side, cocking my hip out, my hands becoming aggressive as I spoke, "She made this mess and I'm cleaning it up. The least she could do is not be a pain in the ass while I save her sorry hide." I swore if my mother even thought about trying to make a deal with me to get the words to the ritual all bets were off. There wouldn't be enough of her left to rule the Seelie Court let alone survive.

"Now, pet." Chess placed a hand on my arm, his hand on my skin calming some of my anger. "We can't just kill the queen because she is being nasty. No matter how warranted."

I frowned at him. I didn't want to be calm, I wanted to be angry, and his touch was projecting his emotions onto me. I could tell this whole feeling what I'm feeling thing was going to get annoying fast.

"Plus you promised not to, remember?" I turned my frown toward Alice. I had promised that, hadn't I? Damn it all to hell and back.

"Fine. No maiming of the queen. Happy?" I glanced around the room and then sighed. "But that doesn't change the fact that we still need the words to the ritual to get rid of them, and we aren't going to get those here." I paused for a moment and then remembered the compact Pat had given me. I would think that someone who was used to using a cell phone would remember something so similar in their pocket. My hand reached into my pocket only to come up empty.

I looked to Alice, confusion on my face. "What happened to the mirror Pat gave me?"

This time it was Alice's turn to frown. Sadness filled her eyes as she held out her hand to show me the compact and all of its pieces in her hand. The mirror had been smashed, the hinge that combined the top and bottom pulled apart.

"It fell out of your pocket when you collapsed. We tried to magic it back together, but it seems to need a different sort of touch." She glanced at Hatter for support. "Maybe Pat could still fix it? Or make a new one?"

"We don't have time to go all the way back to Pat's, we need to contact my mother now." I turned to Hatter, impatience starting to color my words. "Don't you have a mirror here?"

He shook his head, his silver hair shaking back and forth. "Not one that can be used as a portal, or even as a communication device. I do not wish to deal with the Higher Fae any more than I have to." His mouth twisted into a grimace.

"Well, there goes that idea," I groaned.

"We could just go to my house." Chess stepped forward. His tail released my leg and I instantly missed the touch. He glanced back at me with a knowing smile that made me blush before he flicked his hair over his shoulder and shrugged. "If it's still there, that is. I haven't been there in a while, who knows what has happened since I've been gone."

"It's worth a shot either way. We don't have anywhere else to go, and your place is closer than Seer's." I gave a half shrug, not really happy with the plan, but there wasn't much else we could do. We couldn't run back and forth between the realms, not without eventually running into the Shadows, and talking to my mother via mirror was safer than seeing her in person. Either way, we weren't going to get anywhere hanging around Hatter's house.

THE TRIP FROM Hatter's to Chess' was a lot less scary with another Fae besides Mop and Trip by my side. We had decided it was best for Alice to stay with Hatter. Well, I decided that, because she seemed to want to so badly, and I didn't have the heart to tell her no. Besides, what could she do anyways? Glamour the Shadows to death?

The walk was quiet and peaceful. If we hadn't been in the middle of a war, I'd have said it was almost like a date. Two people strolling through the woods, their hands brushing every once in a while as they snuck secret looks at each other. It was kind of fun, that was until we reached the Willow Tree.

I could tell right away something was wrong. The leaves of the tree were dried up, and most of them had fallen to the ground. There was no movement in the tree when we approached. The vines stayed where they were instead of sweeping open like a curtain to welcome us in, and the inside wasn't any better.

The green grass that almost glowed with different colored mushrooms was brown and patchy, with no fungi in sight. The trail that led up to Chess' throne was all but nonexistent, and what was worse than the decay around us, was the figure sitting in Chess' spot.

"What do we have here?" Dorian sat on the throne, one leg thrown over the side almost exactly the same way Chess' had been the first time we met. Except, Chess didn't have a grin on his face so malevolent that it sent chills down my spine.

He still looked like Dorian, black clothing on top of black boots. His dark hair braided in small areas. Even the blue of his eyes was the same. To any onlooker, they would think there was nothing wrong with him, but it was his aura. His very presence was different.

The further he came into the light, the more I felt it press down on me. He wasn't even trying, and the darkness in him was leaking all over the place. How had he gotten so much power so fast? Surely the Shadows couldn't be powerful enough to make him feel this way. That's when I realized it.

They didn't give him anything. He hadn't joined their side; he had become their side. That grin on his face wasn't one that Dorian would have ever worn, but the Shadow man would. That sort of 'I'm thinking about what you look like on the side' kind of gaze that made my skin buzz with energy.

Chess' need to protect me billowed up inside me, and it almost made me smile, but I held it back not wanting to give Dorian any ammunition to use against us.

"What do you want?" I stepped forward, not giving Chess the chance to stand between us, one more moment and he would have done just that.

The laugh that came out of Dorian was not his laugh. It burned along my skin like an icy chill. There was so much power; so much evil in that laugh, it made my determination die a little bit. How was I supposed to win? I wasn't strong enough.

A warm hand slipped into mine and my head cleared. The hopelessness I was feeling disappeared, and I gave Chess a thankful smile. That had been the wrong thing to do, because not soon after, Dorian let out a roar that shook the ground.

"No!" he yelled, gripping his hair in his hands. "You promised me they wouldn't be together. That she would be mine!" His face jerked to the side and then the other like he was fighting some kind of internal battle before all of a sudden he stopped, and his wicked grin fell back into place.

"Tell me, my love." The endearment on his lips was like a worm crawling along my skin, and I fought not to rub my arms to be rid of it. "Has our dear Cheshire told you why he has been beaten and offered up to Fae of all kinds for his playmates?"

My brow scrunched down, what was he getting at? "Because he's a half-breed and the moderator."

Dorian shook a finger at us, making a tut-tutting noise with his tongue. "Someone's been telling tall tales. Get it?" his eyes lit up with laughter. "Tails? Because he's a cat!"

"Get to the fucking point, Dorian." I snarled, not liking where he was going with this conversation, I could already feel the unease in Chess, and it didn't sit well.

His laughter didn't die off; it just stopped, all at once. In the place of laughter was a nasty grin. "Let me tell you a story, shall I?" he didn't wait for anyone to answer. He crossed one leg over the other he floated in the air before us. "Once upon a time, a scared queen wanted to get rid of all the bad little Fae who were terrorizing her kingdom. So, instead of doing the civil thing and putting them out of their misery, she decided to put them in a place no one would miss them. The Shadow Realm."

"We know all this already, you are trying my patience," I said through clenched teeth, my hand tightening around Chess'.

"Now, now do not get so huffy." He waved me off as if I were a fly buzzing around his head, and then his lip poked out in a pout. "We are just now getting to the best part."

"You aren't telling us anything new." Chess growled his apprehension to leave making me sick to my stomach.

"No." my voice made Chess quickly look to me. "I want to know what he has to say."

"Why? He's just going to lie and twist things to how he wants them." He gestured toward Dorian, who was sitting patiently in midair, happy as a peach to see us fight.

I didn't tell him I could feel his terror, he knew I could. But I also wanted to know what he had been so desperate to keep from me after we had promised no more secrets. I wasn't sure Chess would tell me the truth if I asked now.

"Go on, then." I gestured my head toward Dorian, urging him to continue. "Tell me what you want me to hear, so you can get out of my face."

"Very well, I will get it over with." Suddenly, his glee was replaced with anger. "The reason your dear ol' Cheshire was tortured and pimped out was because your mother was trying to get the last ingredient for her little spell."

"Ingredient?" I asked the question, though I knew what he was talking about. She had told me before I wasn't ready to do the spell, and when she took Chess, she had left a note telling me *now* I was ready, but then I didn't know what she meant. The combination of Chess' mumbled words about hearts and ploy to marry me off to Dorian to produce a half-breed led to only one conclusion. Standing in front of Dorian with an apprehensive Chess at my side, I knew all too well what that last ingredient was.

"Love," I said quietly, I dropped Chess' hand at the realization. "The last ingredient is love."

"Correct!" Dorian clapped his hands together sharply. "And who do you think was in charge of getting that last ingredient once the queen found out who you were?"

I stared at the ground hard not wanting to look to the side and see the guilt on Chess' face. I could feel it well enough, like a sickness building in my soul. It had been a game all along. I had been a fool to believe him after he had denied me the first time. Why did I think a little magical exchange mixed with some mind-blowing sex would make him love me?

"No more secrets, huh?" I scoffed and jerked away when he reached out to touch me. I didn't want to calm down. I didn't want him anywhere near me.

"You have to understand. I didn't tell you because I didn't want to hurt you," Chess pleaded with me, his eyes large and full of sorrow.

"But he did hurt you, didn't he?" Dorian pranced between us, a smile lighting up his face. He was delighted to have caused our pain and was trying his best to rub our faces in it. I was about ready to rub his face in something else.

"I don't know if I can do this anymore." I shook my head, ignoring the overwhelming need to punch Dorian in the face. My heart was breaking all over again and I was tired. Tired of fighting, tired of being the one in charge, and most of all, I was tired of feeling.

I could feel Chess' anguish and regret. It was under my skin, and I felt myself choking on it. His was overriding my own feelings of hurt and betrayal. It should have made me see reason. It should have made me realize how sorry he was, but all it did was infuriate me.

The angrier I became, the more distraught his feelings were, and I couldn't take it anymore. I couldn't even feel what I wanted to feel without him raining all over me. I needed a break. I needed to breathe. So I did the only thing I could do. I ran.

CHAPTER 15

ONE LAST MESSAGE

A HOLE BEGAN to open up inside me the farther I ran from them. It widened and stretched and forced my run from a sprint to a slow trot. If this was what it was going to be like every time Chess and I separated, I didn't know how we were going to be able to live without each other.

I could still feel his pain. His wallowing despair that ate me up inside and told me the Shadows had not killed him after I left. It was a small blessing, but also just as much a curse. I couldn't handle my own emotions half the time, I didn't know if I could deal with both of ours at once. There had to be some way to shield myself from him. Some way to have some peace.

At that thought, I took a moment to take in where I had ended up. Running in the Underground wasn't like running in the human world. You might run down the same road every day and the scenery would never change, but here, things were ever changing and moving. If someone had ever made a map of the UnSeelie Court, it would change before you got a chance to use it.

Twisted trees with leafless branches lined the path. Darkness and an eerie calm filled the area. As my feet hit the dirt, a creeping dread accompanied the hole inside me. I knew where I was, but how I had gotten here was a mystery.

The Veil of the Faeries was not a pleasant place to be. The last time I had been here I'd been attacked by a horde of nasty little bug-like creatures. Though, if there were any kind of bug in the human world that could argue with you and call you names, we'd be in a world of trouble.

My feet moved on their own as if they knew something I did not, while the rest of me was tense and cautious of any faeries waiting in the brush. If I was lucky, they were still in the human world causing havoc. I'd been unlucky a lot lately, and I wanted to be prepared.

As I made my way down the path with nothing jumping out at me, my shoulders began to relax and that creeping dread all but disappeared. When I wasn't running for my life, the place was actually not that bad. A few sprinklers and a good gardener, and it would be good to go, that was until a familiar tree came into view.

The last time I had seen the talking tree it had been decaying with only enough energy to talk to me through a dream, and even then, it had been overtaken by the Shadows. Now standing before it, I knew without even asking that the tree was good and truly dead.

Its bark was blackened and dry, its branches no longer held fruit or leaves. I couldn't feel any life coming from the tree and wondered how in the world it had ended up here. I stood there staring at the tree, not sure what to do, or where to go from here.

My feet had other ideas. I stumbled as they were forced forward and toward the tree. I held my hands out in front of me as they led me right up to the trunk. It was a good thing I had, because my feet didn't stop until I was good and pressed against the base of the tree. The moment I touched the tree, I knew that I had been wrong about it.

It wasn't dead. Not completely. It was barely hanging on and was using the last of its energy just to get me there. To show me one last thing. How I knew this I could only guess, it was projecting into my mind, like it had so many times before. Though, this time it was different, when it entered my mind to show me what it needed me to see, it wasn't a whole complete picture.

Jumbled images invaded my mind, and they were so sharp, so severe that they caused me to wince. The images were of my friends, Mop and Trip, even Chess was there. They were being absorbed by the Shadows, their very beings joining the collective of Fae that made up the forgotten Fae. The worst part was the face of the Shadows. It still held Dorian's body captive as it used him as a puppet for its own games.

It was a warning. What I could expect if I failed. Like I needed it. I knew what was at stake, but what I didn't know was why they would waste their last bit of energy to remind me?

Do not...

I jumped in place, my hand still on the base of the tree as the words whispered through my head, pained and so quiet I could scarcely hear.

...let...your love...get in the way.

"Don't let love get in the way?" I asked out loud and shook my head. "But how can I do that, when love is the final ingredient for the spell?"

I didn't get an answer for that one at first, and then when it did speak, it wasn't the answer I was looking for.

Love...will...win.

And then it was gone. It was like a rush of wind had come out of the tree. Maybe its soul was leaving? Did trees even have souls?

I stepped back from the tree. My feet crunched on the dirt beneath my feet. It didn't make sense, any of it. Don't let love get in the way, but love will win? It was a complete contradiction.

A flapping from behind me pulled me around to see Seer landing on the ground a few feet away. For once, she was wearing something modest and that didn't scream sex. Her six arms came out the sides of a long, pale blue maxi dress. Her feet were bare, while her periwinkle blue hair was left wild and untamed. Her pale blue face had a hint of red, and her breathing came in pants as she placed one of her hands over her heart.

"Where have you been? I have been looking for you everywhere," she said between breaths, her vibrant, cerulean wings sagging behind her.

"Here." I shrugged gesturing around me with a frown. "Why were you looking for me?"

"I had a vision of you facing the Shadows, and then something about a gaping hole." She made a confused face and clasped my hands in hers. "It sent everyone into a panic. We didn't know where you were or if you had failed. When Chess came to me, I could tell something was wrong, but he wouldn't say."

I looked away from her inquiring eyes and wrapped my arms around myself tightly. I knew why he was upset. Being this far away didn't keep me from being able to feel his pain. To know how sorry he was for what he had done. He wanted to make up for his mistake, and I wanted him too. He so easily lied to my face before and I didn't feel a thing. How could I trust he wouldn't do it again?

"Lady?" Seer placed a hand on my arm, and I turned my gaze to her, not liking the pity in her eyes. "Whatever has happened between you two can be fixed. You can't let the Shadows win."

Suspicion crept in and my eyes narrowed at her. "I thought you didn't know what happened?"

She gave a small, nonchalant shrug. "Sometimes it's better to let others tell me than to let on all that I've seen. Most people don't particularly like me to be in their personal business."

"I can imagine," I muttered, pulling away from her to put some distance between the tree and me. It couldn't help me anymore, and being here just felt morbid. Like I was hanging out by someone's grave.

"Where are you going now?" Seer's words followed me, her feet padding along the ground. "We really shouldn't stay here. The others are waiting."

"Others?"

A slight breeze ruffled my hair as her wings flapped. I glanced to the side where Seer landed. "Yes, others. Don't you want to see your friends? They are all waiting for you back at my home." One of her main hands gestured toward where I could only assume she lived.

"Of course I do, but I have to talk to my mother. I need to end this once in for all."

My feet kept moving, not worried about her keeping up. She could fly if she got tired, or she could just hover.

"Yes, yes. Don't worry. I have a mirror back at my place, you can contact her from there, but really, Lady," she paused her dark eyes searching around her, a wariness in her voice. "We really shouldn't loiter here."

This time I stopped. "That is the second time you have tried to get us out of here. While I don't disagree, it's pretty creepy. It doesn't look like the faeries are home. So what gives?"

She visibly gulped and lowered her voice as she leaned into me. "There is a reason only the faeries live here and why everything is so..." her gaze flittered around. "...dead."

"Then why don't you tell me," I whispered back, annoyance starting to inch up in my voice.

If she noticed, she didn't say, her attention was too focused on the world around us. "This is a graveyard. Not just because of the dead plants, but this is where all Fae come when they die."

"I thought Fae couldn't die. That you were immortal?"

"Bah." She made a face. "You know better than to think that, you died."

"Yeah, but that was caused by magical forces, it's not the same thing." I held my hands up with a shake of my head. "And Chess already said you couldn't starve, well not right away anyways. It would take a long time, like centuries."

"See, we can still die." She pointed a finger at me. "And there are other things too. We might heal fast but you could still kill one of us with iron or a good chop to the head." Her hand sliced down in front of her as she demonstrated. "Then the remains are burned and brought here."

I stared down at the dusty gray ground and had a sudden urge to jump up onto a rock or something. Who knew whose remains I was standing on? That still didn't explain why we needed to leave so quickly.

"I see you will not take my word for it." She sighed, a bit irritably, shaking her head. "I'm surprised you have lasted this long without dying because of your stubbornness."

"I'm not stubborn. I'm just not an idiot who believes everything anyone tells me," I said, defensively.

"That remains to be seen." Her eyes lit with laughter and then her face sobered.

"The faeries feed on the ashes of the fallen Fae, and in turn, they produce a sort of substance that can be harvested and put into our wines. In a way, we are taking back in the Fae who have left us, which is why humans get intoxicated quickly on it. There is a buildup of leftover magic in each drink, that shouldn't be ingested by mere mortals."

"Ew." My nose wrinkled, and I had the urge to wash my mouth out with soap. I was never drinking faerie wine again. Circle of life or not, that was just disgusting.

"But that's not all." She shook a finger at me, silencing my disgust. "Fae aren't like humans whose souls know where to go when they die, they have to be coaxed out. Thus, why we burn the remains to make them seem less attractive."

I nodded my head like it made sense. The Fae were self-absorbed and shallow in life, why should they be any different in death? At least humans had the decency to know when you are down to stay down.

"So where do the souls go?"

"Ah, that's the thing. They don't go anywhere. They stay here." She swept an arm around the veil. "Another job of the faeries is to make sure the spirits stay here, so that when the Reaper comes by they will be ready for him."

"Reaper?"

It was her turn to nod, her hair falling over her face. "Yes, and no one knows when he will come by, so, it is best for us to be on our way and not get in his way."

"Why? What will happen?" I cocked my head to the side, curiosity eating at me. I had heard talk of the Reaper before. My mother had made a deal with him to get rid of the Shadows. That obviously didn't go over too well, and if I saw him, I'd like to have a word or two with him for making the deal in the first place.

"How should I know?" Befuddlement caused her brows to bunch together between her eyes. "No one has been here when he came —at least no one that survived to tell the tale."

"But what—" I started, but a sudden chill overcame me. It wasn't like my mother's icy glare, where it was sharp and meant to hurt. Or like the Shadows where they couldn't help the magic leaking off of them when they spoke causing your insides to freeze. This was a different kind of cold.

The kind that made the hairs on the back of your neck stand up but when you turned around no one was there. This was a feeling that made you want to go screaming into the darkness, because whatever was coming was so much worse.

It was that very feeling that kept me from arguing when Seer grabbed my hand and said, "Run."

CHAPTER 16

THOSE WE FOUGHT FOR

I RAN FOR the second time in less than an hour, but this time I had a reason to run.

Seer pulled on my hand, trying to make me go faster. I could tell by the fluttering of her wings that she wanted to take flight but couldn't, because I was slowing her down. I almost told her to go on without me. The cold that I had felt seemed to trek after us as if seeking out our warmth. If it caught up with us, I didn't want to be found on my own.

We were almost to the woods; the trees were just a few yards away. I pushed myself to go faster, though my lungs burned and my knees ached. Just as we were about to cross the line of the trees, the cold feeling turned into a numbing sensation. I saw something out of the corner of my eye, it reached out to touch my shoulder. Before I could turn to see what it was, we crossed the trees and the presence faded away.

Seer collapsed against a tree, her wings hanging down to the ground as she caught her breath. I fell to the ground, not caring if I was getting myself dirty. My eyes were on where we had come from, where all was silent and nothing moved. Just how close to death had I been?

"Best not to dwell on it." Seer moved away from her leaning post and held a hand out to me. I gave one more cursory look toward the veil before placing my hand in hers, letting her pull me to my feet.

I let her lead as we made our way through the dark forest. The night had begun to wane and light poured through the treetops. The forest changed from dark and ominous to gray and dreary. Cheerful really wasn't a word that could ever be used to describe it.

"Where are we going?" I kept pace with Seer as she maneuvered through the trees and over branches like an old pro.

She didn't slow down or turn to me as she spoke, "Back to my home. Everyone is waiting for you."

"But can we get there through the forest?" I swept an arm around me, the forest not letting up the further we walked. "I went through the hedge maze the last time and that isn't anywhere close to here."

Seer snorted and rolled her eyes. "That's because you came the back way. Not like it matters, you know how fickle the Underground can be. North might be north one day but the next it could be south." She crossed her arms to demonstrate. "You try giving directions when your home keeps moving on you. The only place that doesn't seem to move is the palace. Probably some kind of trick to it but of course the queens aren't sharing." Bitterness dripped from her voice as she frowned, but then she turned to me with a smile. "But that will all change once you are queen, won't it?"

I winced at the question. Queen. How did I tell her that I would never be queen? At least not until my mother stepped down, not that she would, or I wanted her to. I had no intentions of being queen, even if given the chance. I was happy enough to stay in the human world where at least I could find my house without a magical low jack on it.

Seer's smile lowered at my expression. "What is it? You do want to be queen, don't you? The people are already loyal to you on both sides. You could be Queen of the whole Underground with a snap of your fingers and no one would argue the point."

"My mother would," I interjected. "You know she won't give up her power to anyone, not even her daughter. Besides, I don't think I would make a very good queen. I can't even keep a job." I shook my head at the memory of the one job I had gotten since moving back from New York.

Everyone told me going to school for English Literature was a bad idea. They'd said I'd never find a job. And they were right. Unless I wanted to be a writer, or had an in with a publishing house, the only other options were being a teacher or a librarian. The last option was the one I had been reduced to when I came back to Iowa and I'd already lost that job because of the whole Fae fiasco.

It was hard to keep a full-time job and save the world. Just ask Superman! Then again Superman could move at the speed of light and didn't have a snotty mean girl for a boss.

"Pfft." Three hands waved me off. "Don't sell yourself so short. Maybe you aren't good at the human jobs because you were meant for something else? Something magical? Hmm?" her eyebrows rose as she gave me a knowing look. "You'll never know until you try."

I chewed on my lip, and not wanting to burst her bubble, I gave a noncommittal answer, "We'll see."

"That's right we will!" her hands clapped together and her face lit up with glee before three hands stopped and pointed. "Look, we are almost there!"

An archway in front of us made of two trees that had been bent and twisted into each other stood a few paces ahead. On the outside of the trees there was just more forest, but through the opening of the arch, vibrant, multicolored mushrooms grew from the ground. I didn't know how long it had been there or if it just magically appeared. Either way, I probably would have never found it on my own.

As we approached the arch, I let Seer take the lead. Cowardly? Probably. But I'd learned my lesson about going head first into doorways on my own, and while I could see what was on the other side, I still didn't completely trust the magic of the Underground. Jaded? Who me?

"Come now, let's get you back. We have to contact the queen as soon as possible." Seer stepped through the archway, and when she didn't immediately disappear, and was still there on the other side surrounded by mushrooms, I stepped through after her.

When my feet went from dirt to cushy green grass the hole in my heart grew just a little bit smaller, and I knew I was close to Chess. I followed after Seer, and with each step, my heart thudded harder and my hands began to sweat.

Why was I nervous? It wasn't like I hadn't seen Chess in a while. Yes, we had just declared our love to each other, and then he went and lied to me, but I also didn't stay to let him explain. I shouldn't be this nervous, he should be. That's when I realized, it wasn't just me, but it was Chess too.

He must have sensed me the moment I got closer like I had, and like with the hole, the closer we got the more strongly we felt the other's feelings. So my nervousness ended up being amplified by his. God, I couldn't imagine how this would affect our day to day lives, let alone if we had kids!

I couldn't help but smile a bit at that thought. While having little Chesses running around sounded like a good idea, it tickled me that for once Chess would be able to understand what childbirth was like — and cramps! God, I forgot about those.

My thoughts made the nervous jitters lessen and mild curiosity came from Chess. He was probably wondering what the hell I was thinking about to be so amused.

Seer walked beside me oblivious to the inner exchange of emotions between Chess and I. I had been walking slowly alongside her when all of a sudden; a sharp pang of need hit me. My feet sped up, and I found myself power walking, almost on the verge of running. It took all that I had to keep myself from sprinting toward where Chess was like a beacon in the night.

My eyes finally landed on a group of Fae, like those I had seen through the mirror, but there were way more than I had initially thought. I scanned the crowd, even as my magic kept moving me toward my other half. Even through the pulsing need, I was able to make out a few new creatures I'd never seen before.

Frog and fish like creatures stood on two legs with waistcoats. A turtle with an eyeglass and top hat stood beside a hound dog that was quieting his pups. As I made my way through the crowd, all eyes turned to me, and a rush of self-consciousness filled me.

That aching need was only getting stronger the further I went, and I felt like there was a huge neon sign pointing at me. Letting everyone there know just how desperate I was to get to Chess. My face heated as I imagined exactly what they smelled.

I thought about using my magic to mask my scent, but that would point an even bigger finger at me. So, instead, I kept my eyes forward and tried not to think about all the eyes on me. When Mop stepped out of the crowd to greet me, I even bypassed him and kept going. He was probably frowning at my back, but I couldn't be forced to care, all thoughts were on fulfilling the want inside me.

A movement in the crowd in front of me caught my attention. Fae were being pushed aside left and right, and I could catch a glimpse of pale pink hair and a twitching ear in between each movement. Eventually, the crowd took the hint and parted, revealing a ferocious feline that froze me in place.

The curiosity in him had faded and his desire reached out and caressed mine and it caused it to flare even brighter. The intensity of it made me gasp and my insides clench. The world around us faded, and I couldn't see anyone but him.

I waited with desperate anticipation as he took one step after the other until he was standing in front of me. He didn't say anything, and though we were both consumed with our need, I could feel his need to apologize in the back of my throat. I think I nodded, or maybe I just thought it, but the next thing I knew his mouth was on mine.

If the crowd was watching us I wouldn't have known, my hands buried in his hair and my front pressed tightly against his as we tried to meld ourselves together. His clawed hands gripped the sides of my arms, almost tight enough to break the skin. I heard a loud groan and realized with a start that it came from me. The haze that had been clouding my mind faded, and I quickly took the opportunity to get a grip on myself.

My hands loosened in his silky tresses and moved to push against his steel chest still pressed against mine. Chess didn't take the hint. He was too wrapped up in the desire to be closer to me. My magic built up, and I pressed it toward him, just to give him a little zap, but all that did was send a wave of pleasure between us. It was like he was inside me, caressing parts that should never be touched, and it almost caused me to lose my grip again.

Thankfully, someone cleared their throat, reminding me once more that we weren't alone. It was what I needed to finally rip myself away from Chess, and my eyes popped open. I kept my gaze on Chess' face not daring to look at those around us. My face was already as red as a tomato. I didn't think it could get any worse, but I didn't want to take the chance.

My reluctance to participate anymore caused the grip on my shoulders to lessen and Chess opened his green orbs. His eyes were still a bit clouded, but there was just a hint of him still in there that told me he was closer to himself than before.

"Hi," I breathed. He smiled until just a hint of fang was showing.

"Hello, pet." His hands smoothed down the sides of my arms, rubbing them in a comforting motion. My embarrassment lessened a bit at the movement and I returned his smile.

"I'm glad you are okay." I chewed on my lip and peered up at him with uncertainty. "I was worried he might have done something to you when I left."

Bitterness hit me like a sledgehammer to the chest and it made me stumble. Chess' hands grabbed me before I could fall and the bitterness turned to concern.

"We really need to get a hold on this or we are going to go crazy." I shook my head at him, there was no need to explain what this was his agreement was clear enough.

A throat cleared once again, this time with annoyance from its owner. We turned toward the sound to see Mop standing beside us, irritation on his brown face. His arms were crossed and his foot tapped, he was the only one out of all the Fae who had the audacity to be mad at us when the rest of them were either embarrassed, pretending not to watch, or had hunger in their eyes.

"Sorry, Mop. I didn't mean to ignore you, I was just…preoccupied." My gaze slid to Chess who shot me an emotion so intense I had to close my eyes for a moment to catch my breath. I threw him an annoyed look that I knew he could feel as well but he replied with a cheeky grin.

"That!" Mop shouted, his short pudgy finger pointing at us. "What ya'll be doin'?"

I shuffled my feet and tucked a strand of hair behind my ear. "It's complicated."

Mop snorted and then leaned in close to sniff the air in front of him. "That complication be havin' to do with why the cat be smellin' like ye?"

My eyebrows rose and I had a sudden urge to sniff Chess and then myself in return. Weirdly, Chess didn't seem surprised that we smelled the same. Did our exchange of magic cause it? I wouldn't have thought that it would change our scents, but with my limited knowledge of magic, I shouldn't be surprised.

"Lady!" an ecstatic voice called out and a familiar pair of floppy ears came into view followed by the rest of the hopping opalaught. "Lady, Trip missed Lady, Trip did!"

A smile spread across my face, and I kneeled down until I was eye level with him. Holding my arms out to him for a hug, I couldn't help but bury my face into his fur as we embraced. I might complain about the Underground, but one thing I couldn't get enough of was this little fur ball and his forever innocent and cheerful nature.

"I missed you too, Trip." I squeezed him tight and then pulled him away. "But you shouldn't be here. None of you should." I let my eyes scan over the crowd.

"But we wanted to help Lady, we did." Trip frowned, his ears falling down around his face, his sadness tugging at my heart.

Mop stepped forward, placing a hand on my shoulder. "We be wantin' ye to know ye ain't alone in this. We be willin' to fight for ye since it be our home ye be fightin' for. Ye don' be havin' to go at it alone."

My gaze softened at the brownie, not expecting such a speech from him. It was almost not grumpy at all. At the beginning of all this I would have been delighted to take him up on that offer but since then I'd learned the hard way what it meant to be up against the Shadows. If I took them into battle I wouldn't just be gaining an army, I'd be giving Dorian targets to use against me. I had no doubt that he would stoop so low, the Shadows had.

"While I appreciate the offer, Mop. This is really something I have to do alone." I placed my hand on top of his, giving it a reassuring pat. "I would feel more secure if I knew you were somewhere safe away from all of this." I gave him a teasing smile. "Besides, I met your wife and that is not a woman who would stay a widow long, should you not come back."

"Well, I...uh..." Mop sputtered, his face turning red as he stared down at his shoes.

Having mercy I turned my attention back to the creature in my arms. "And you…" I tapped Trip on the nose with a smile. "I need you to take care of Alice and my garden, in case I don't come back."

"Don't say that, Lady, don't." he shook his head sadly, his tail swaying behind him as he clung to me. "Lady's carrots are the best, no way can Trip compare, no way."

"I'm sure you will get the hang of it, but that's only *if* things go wrong. That doesn't mean I won't go down without a fight." I put my fists up to show him I was ready for anything, but he didn't smile, if anything, his expression fell further. Letting out a sigh, I patted him on the head before standing to my feet.

Twisting around to where Seer was standing off to the side waiting I asked, "Are you ready?"

Glancing around the area, and then to Chess who held his hand out to me. I clasped mine in his and turned back to her. "Let's go."

CHAPTER 17

WORDS AND BLOOD

THE MIRROR SEER brought us to was not the one that led to the Shadows Between. It was a smaller, square shaped one that was a little ways away from the crowd of Fae.

They didn't run and hide like I had tried to urge them. They seemed dead set on seeing this through, even if it was from afar. They wanted to be there together no matter what happened.

I couldn't fault them. If the fate of my world was narrowed down to one ex-librarian that didn't really belong anywhere, I'd be a little nervous too. Hell, I was nervous because it was me. Dear God, don't let me fuck this up.

I reached my hand up to touch the frame of the mirror, my mother at the forefront of my mind, but my hand was stopped by Chess'. I turned to him with a questioning look. He gave my hand a small squeeze and smiled.

"Let's do it together."

My lips tipped up and I nodded. Chess drew my hand up until we touched the frame of the mirror. The surface rippled and churned longer than usual. At first, I thought it wouldn't give us what we wanted. Did we think two different things? Was she not near a mirror? But then the mirror stopped and the image of my mother sitting at her vanity appeared.

She was alone without her guards or servants. Her head was down and she was staring hard at something in her hands. I squinted to see what it was.

It was a tiny cloth doll with blue hair and cream-colored skin. It wore a little red dress that didn't go with her hair at all. She had a stitch on one arm where she had caught it on the thorn bush in the gardens. I knew because it was my doll she was holding.

My nanny at the time had given it to me as a gift, and I had taken it everywhere. I loved that doll more than anything else and when she had gotten a tear, I had made the mistake of running to my mother begging her to fix it. She had scoffed at me looking at the doll with disgust.

"Princesses should not play with silly toys such as this." She had grabbed it from me and thrown it to one of the guards. "Get rid of it."

I had begged and pleaded with her to let me keep it, but she just sent me to my room. As I cried myself to sleep that night, I had learned a hard lesson about my mother. That was the day I vowed I'd never be like her, and I never asked her for anything ever again.

Except for today. "Hello, Mother."

Her head jerked up from the doll, surprise filling her face before it smoothed into her usual icy stare. "Daughter, I wasn't expecting you so soon. I see you got your cat back, well done." She nodded her head toward Chess, who pressed the front of his body against my side.

It was a comfort to have him so close, but it was also distracting. The magic in me that called out to his was getting restless. We had placated it when we kissed, but it wasn't nearly enough. I shoved it back down like bile rising in my throat and fixated all my attention on the woman in the mirror.

"Yes, the queen helped us out with that." Let her think I had Mab on my side. It wasn't a complete lie.

"Oh?" Her eyebrows rose. "I didn't know she was seeing visitors already. My visit must have cheered her up more than I thought. Well, good for her." The words were meant to be kind but they were tinged with anger.

What had happened between them? I didn't ask. It would be a waste of time. I was lucky to get the answers to important questions, let alone those that were just for curiosity's sake.

"I'm not calling to chat about the family."

"Really? Then what, pray tell, are you bothering me in my private quarters for?" she sat up further in her chair, smoothing her hands over her gown. This one was not like her usual attire. It was a dark blue that was loose and floated down below the vanity top. Her hair wasn't in a complicated do; it fell down around her shoulders. Had I caught her before she was going to bed?

Ignoring the need to ask, I lifted my chin to meet her eyes. "I want the words."

For a moment she didn't answer, she watched me with careful consideration before she asked, "What words?"

Annoyance stabbed at me, and I gave Chess a look that said to calm down. It wouldn't do for us to screw this up when we were so close.

"No more games, Mother. You know what I want." I chose my words carefully, happy that my voice came out steady and confident.

Sniffing, she closed her eyes briefly before picking up her brush from the vanity. She slid the bristles over her hair in slow, precise movements. Each stroke a calculated movement. She was thinking so hard I swore I could almost hear her thoughts. She was considering not giving them to me, or at least not without a fight.

The realization caused a rage in me that made my magic spark to life. The magic in Chess responded, in turn, brushing along my skin where his body pressed against mine. The combination caused a volatile reaction that caused the mirror to crackle and shake.

It must have affected the mirror on her side, because her eyes snapped up and her brush paused mid-brush. There was a hint of fear in her eyes that made part of me smile. She was finally realizing that her fears of me were true.

"The words, Mother," I said slowly, with a hint of violence in my voice.

Setting the brush down, her lips pressed firmly together like she wanted to say something but was holding back. She placed her hands on top of the vanity and drew her shoulders back as if prepping herself for a role.

"You must say these words exactly or it will not work. It is a variation of a blood oath, and if you don't get the wording right, then they might find a way to wiggle out of it, and then we'll be right back where we started."

I didn't have to ask who they were. If you gave them a chance to manipulate your words then they would do it in a heartbeat. If she said I had to say them exactly, then that was what I was going to do.

"Understood." I nodded, letting her know I was ready.

"Blood of like blood, my heart to yours, return to the realm from which you came and dwell here no longer." As she said the words a chill spread along my skin, causing goose bumps to rise.

I held back the urge to rub them away, and instead, focused on remembering the words. Blood of like blood? Was it because I was a half-breed and that sort of made us the same? Neither of us belonged to one world, but the Shadows belonged more to the Shadow Realm than any other world anyways.

The second part, my heart to yours, didn't sit well. What did that mean? Could that be the part that Chess warned me about that could cause me to die? I hoped not.

The last part was fairly obvious. It was demanding them to go back to where they came from. But what if what they thought they came from was this world and not the Shadow Realm? Would that be enough for them to change the deal?

The words obviously held power from just her saying them. So, would they be even more powerful when combined with blood? I couldn't say I looked forward to that part.

"Where did you get the spell from?" Chess spoke up beside me, his unease pressing onto me. At least I wasn't the only one unsure about the words.

My mother wasn't surprised by the question and simply shrugged. "Oh, around."

"That's likely." The sarcasm dripped from my words as I frowned. "It's a fair question. I don't want to be saying something I don't know for sure will work. How do I know you aren't just sending me to my death?"

It was her turn to frown. She made an audible noise in the back of her throat and then picked up the doll she had discarded.

"I might not have been the best of mothers." I snorted and she glared at me. "But, whether or not you believe it, I've always had your interest at heart. Maybe after this is all over we could start over and have the kind of relationship you always wanted?"

I was taken aback by the hopefulness in her voice. She wanted a relationship with me? Her? The one who had spent my whole life shutting me out and then keeping me from anyone else that could possibly influence me to think the wrong way? I didn't think so.

"Yeah, maybe. If I don't die in the process," I said instead of what I was thinking.

Dropping the doll to the vanity, she sighed. "You aren't going to die, Lynne." The sound of my name on her lips sounded more natural than I wanted to admit.

Chess wasn't fooled by her words, his hand tightened around me. "How do you know?"

"Because, the spell is meant to suck them back into the Shadow Realm. The Reaper gave it to me himself. The only way you would die is if you aren't strong enough to resist the pull." Her condescending attitude was back in full force.

"What pull?" I asked her.

"Of the blood, of course. Saying the words are all fine and dandy but without the blood, it is practically useless. The blood is everything." Her eyes glinted at the mention of blood, a kind of hunger reaching her eyes.

"Is that it?" her hunger was creeping me out, and I wanted nothing more to not see her anymore.

"Don't forget what I said," she said before I could end the call. "We could have the relationship you always wanted. The kind your human mother can't give you."

The mention of my human mother made my blood boil. How dare she even speak of her? If I had a choice between her and the queen, I would choose her every time. My human mother might not be perfect, but at least she hadn't tried to breed me or get me killed.

"I might not be able to remove you from your throne but know this..." My gazed hardened at her. "There will be changes when this is all over. Big changes, and if I am not here to personally see to it." Chess squeezed my hand, a reassuring feeling passing to me. "Chess will make sure my wishes are followed, and remember, he hasn't made any such promise."

My mother's eyes glanced to Chess and back to me. She nodded a bit more vigorously, showing how affected she was by my threat. For the first time ever, my mother looked old. Her eyes were strained and there were lines on her face. It made me wonder if this whole ordeal had aged her, or if she had been using glamour this whole time? I almost pitied her, but then remembered this was her fault in the first place, and I was the one paying the price.

"Good," I continued, "Then we understand one another." I was about to turn away from the mirror but stopped. "And if we never see each other again, you should rethink how you treat others. Right now father is still on your side, but push him too much, and you will end up losing him." I gave her a sad smile. "Immortality is a wondrous and lonely burden to bear."

I watched her expression morph from cautious to anger, and I thought she was going to lash out at me, but she didn't. Instead, she bowed her head slightly. "Thank you. I will take that under advisement."

The mirror cleared and a sense of relief mixed with dread filled me. We had the words, we knew what to do. It was finally time to end it all.

CHAPTER 18

FINAL SHOWDOWN

CHESS AND I left the Seer's home in the Mushroom City with plenty of tears of goodbye, mainly from Trip, and made our way to where we had last seen Dorian. Chess' willow.

When we arrived at the willow it was quiet. The tree that had been withering had all but been destroyed. Chess' throne no longer stood. It was in a million pieces on the ground. Dorian was nowhere in sight.

"Well, where do we go now?" I put my hands on my hips and tapped my foot as I thought. It was too much to hope that Dorian would be where we last saw him. He was no doubt off causing havoc on someone else's life or finding new ways to torture me.

The Shadows, pre-Dorian, were all about pleasing me. Trying to seduce me to their side. But with Dorian thrown into the mix, it seemed like they were fighting for control. He wanted to get me back, but he also wanted me to suffer, well, more like he wanted Chess to suffer, and that just happened to cause me pain in return.

I knew better than to ask Chess where he thought we should go next, his befuddlement was like a blow horn in my head. Sharing emotions made things easier, but it also made it harder to think. While we were apart, the emotions weren't so intense, like a dull roar in the back of my mind, but close like this made it almost impossible to ignore what he was feeling.

I imagined it was the same for him and tried to keep my relief to myself. I knew I was going to have to face Dorian eventually, but could I really be blamed for being relieved that I had a short reprieve, even if it meant I was just delaying the inevitable?

A warm hand covered mine, and I twisted around as Chess brought my hand up to his mouth. He pressed his lips to the underside of my wrist, a small understanding smile on his face. The press of his mouth against my wrist caused a sharp spike of desire and his smile broadened while his eyes darkened. I guess I wasn't that good at hiding my emotions after all.

Gently removing my hand from his, I cleared my throat and looked away. "Since they aren't here anymore we could probably use your mirror to get somewhere else and cut back on the travel time, but I haven't the first clue as to where to go next."

Chess hummed as he thought, his clawed finger tapping his face while his other hand propped against his hip. His pale pink hair had been braided and hung down his back, where his tail swung back and forth in a hypnotic pattern. I pulled my eyes away from his tail in case he thought I was ogling his backside and stepped forward.

"Maybe we should go inside? I don't know about you but standing out here in the open is creeping me out." I started toward the trunk of the tree but was pulled back by Chess' hand on my wrist. I glanced up from my wrist to his emerald eyes. His ears were stiff on top of his head, and a sudden pang of wariness hit me. "What is it?"

"Do you hear that?" His ear twitched again, and his wariness changed to panic just as his eyes widened, and he yelled, "Run!"

Not needing to be told twice, my feet started toward the tree again. I felt it right as we reached the entrance. The ground shook beneath us in a foot pounding rhythm. I gripped the trunk of the willow just to keep from falling over as the shaking increased.

"It's getting closer!" Chess shouted at my side. He was crouched down with his hands on the ground as he tried to keep his balance against the moving earth.

I held onto the tree for dear life. My eyes went to the trees around us. To one side there was a disturbance that was forcing trees to one side. Birds flew out in its wake. I couldn't tell what it was yet, but it was big, and I didn't want to wait to find out.

"How do we get inside?" I pushed against the side of the willow's trunk, trying to find a way into Chess' home, but it wouldn't budge.

Chess crawled up the trunk from his crouched position and pressed his hand against the side. Last time, we had easily walked right through the trunk, but not even Chess' clawed hand could breach the surface of the bark.

"It's not working." He shook his head, panic rising in him, and in turn, spilled into me. "This has never happened before. I don't know why it won't work. Unless..." he trailed off, his eyes as round as saucers. His face scrunched down in an angry frown.

"Unless what?" I probed, the trees closest to us were being shoved aside, and I could see just a hint of a scale and wing. Red eyes gleamed between the trees, locking onto me. A roar caused my heart to stop beating for a moment before I turned back to the tree, banging on it with all my might.

"Open up, you fucking asshole." I kicked and beat at the tree, my hands becoming raw from the bark biting into my skin. Chess grabbed my wrists and forced me to stop, jerking me around to look at him.

"You can't get in that way. The connection is broken." His eyes darted from me to the tree line where the last remaining trees were being pummeled into the ground.

What stepped into the clearing was nothing short of a dragon. Its large wings spanned out at least ten feet each way. Its scale-covered body was three times the size of the JubJub bird, and its claws were so sharp that they dug into the ground with each pounding step it took. If its size wasn't enough to scare the living daylights out of me, the enormous teeth that protruded out of its mouth destroyed any thoughts of trying to reason with the creature.

Chess and I bolted from the tree toward the other side of the clearing. Our feet moved in time as we raced toward safety. Once we hit the trees we'd have a fighting chance. Once we were past the trees we could lose ourselves in the woods and find another way to the Shadows. That is...once we hit the trees.

We never reached the trees. The moment we got around the willow, and down the path on the other side, we screeched to a halt. Dorian stood at the tree line. His hands were behind his back and feet spread apart with a smile that said, "Gotcha."

"Where are you going?" Dorian cocked his head to the side. His dark hair spilled over the side of his face. "Don't you want to meet my new pet?"

"Not particularly." I retorted, not hiding the disdain from my voice.

"What a pity." He pouted and then smiled like he had a new toy he wanted to show off. "I found him wandering around the Between and saved the beast from a life of boredom. He is ever so grateful and will do just about anything for me. Won't you, my little Jabberwocky?"

I grimaced at the tone he used when talking to the beast. One thing I hated more than anything was people who talked to their animals like they were babies. People shouldn't even talk to babies like that, let alone their pets.

At Dorian's appearance, the monstrous beast had stopped its decent onto us. It waited at the base of the willow like a dog waiting did his master's call. Sitting there with its long tail wrapped around its legs, it wasn't quite a terrifying, as it had been when it was chasing us.

I turned away from it and shrugged not impressed. "What can I say? I'm more of a cat person."

A twinge of amusement filled me, and I chanced a glance at Chess, who seemed to be fighting not to smile. Dorian, however, did not find my comment funny. Something dark slid behind his gaze and his smile fell.

A growl reverberated down my spine. Hot air blew against the back of my neck. My body tensed, but I didn't turn. I wouldn't give the jerk the satisfaction of seeing me scared.

"Knock it off, we both know you aren't going to kill me." I crossed my arms with a confident smirk. I was partly bluffing. A part of me hoped that Dorian didn't hate me enough to kill me. That he was still wrapped up in the whole wanting to be with me thing. The Shadows, though, were another story.

They might have wanted me to be their queen at one point, but I was pretty sure they had figured out that there was no chance in hell that I'd be down for that. It was probably why they took Dorian in the first place, to try to appeal to me in a different manner. It hadn't worked, but they got an A for effort.

"Like you are not here to kill me?" he snarled, his hands fisted at his side and rage contorting his face. "Or to send me to the realm from which I came?"

Him quoting back part of the spell threw me through a loop. Had he been spying on us? How else would he know the words of the very spell I was sent here to use on him? So much for the element of surprise.

"So what?" I shrugged, rolling my eyes. "It's not like it was a big secret or anything. I've been telling you since we met that I wouldn't be yours. It is your fault you got it into your head that having Dorian as your puppet would change that."

A sort of ripple ran through Dorian's body, and the anger that was on his face twisted into a disturbing smile. That smile told me that Dorian was no longer with us, and the one looking back out of his eyes was the Shadow man. Creepy and cheerful at the same time, I'd rather face him than my ex any day.

"You are not being completely honest, my queen." His voice hissed along my skin. "I believe when we first met you promised to think about joining us. I do not believe you were being truthful then, either. Now were you?"

"Not really."

He had me there. When I had said I'd think about it, I hadn't actually thought about it. It hadn't even crossed my mind, not seriously anyways. The thought of ruling the Underground was not on my list of aspirations. Getting out of here alive was my top priority right underneath a hot bath and a large glass of wine. Scratch that. Make it a whole bottle of wine.

My response didn't help my cause and his smile curled down. He seemed stumped. As if he couldn't imagine that I would confirm his accusation. Weeks ago, when this all started, I probably would have lied my ass off, but now that it was down to it, I just wanted it over and this was the fastest way there was to piss him off.

"Very well, then." He recovered from his initial confusion and straightened the sleeves of his puffy black shirt. "If you are still determined to be stubborn I suppose I will have to revert to extreme measures."

My stomach sank. I didn't like the sound of that. A roar broke out from behind us. Chess and I stumbled against each other. We clutched onto each other, trying to keep our balance against the shaking ground.

"So, you like cats do you? Maybe after my pet takes care of yours, you will be a bit more open to my offer." I somehow heard Dorian's parting words over the resounding sound and turned my head to argue with him. But a white hole had appeared, seemingly ripped open out of nothing, and he was stepping through it, leaving Chess and me with the rampaging Jabberwocky.

CHAPTER 19

SACRIFICE

I DIDN'T HAVE time to worry about how the hell they had made a hole out of nothing, because I was shoved to the ground by Chess. My mouth got buried in the dirt. I tried to push back up, but Chess kept me pressed down with his body. I turned my head to ask him what the hell when a claw swiped the air above us. The rush of air was right where I had been standing before.

"Thanks." I gasped but didn't have time to say anymore when a shadow appeared above us.

I rolled to the side. The claw slammed down next to me. Scrambling to my feet, I backed away from the Jabberwocky. My eyes swiftly searched out Chess, who had already gotten back to his feet. There wasn't any pain coming from him, but the same panic and disarray in him pumped through me.

"What should we do, pet?" he called out after a particularly loud roar came from the Jabberwocky when he swung at Chess and missed, pushing the feline further away from the hole Dorian had made.

I looked to the hole and back to the Jabberwocky and it clicked. He wasn't just trying to hurt us; he was trying to keep us from following his master. We needed to get to that hole.

I opened my mouth to tell Chess but was hit from behind. I screamed as the scales of the Jabberwocky's tail scrapped my back. I could hear Chess yelling my name as I was thrown across the clearing.

I groaned, my back burning. My head throbbed, and I fought to get back to my feet. Just as I got my bearings, a searing pain scorched my side, bringing me to my knees. I glanced down at where the pain was but nothing was there. There were no tears in the cloth, no blood, nothing.

Another sharp sting to my side, followed by Chess' outcry caused my head to jerk up. The Jabberwocky had gotten a hold of Chess. It gripped him in its claws. The pain wasn't mine. It was Chess'.

Gathering my strength, I did my best to ignore the pain. I pushed myself back to my feet and stumbled toward the dragon creature.

"Hey you!" I called out, grabbing my side as the claws on Chess squeezed harder. The Jabberwocky turned its gaze to me but didn't drop Chess. "Put him down."

"Why human?" the deep crackling voice that replied sent a wave of shock through me.

"You can talk?" I didn't know why the fact that the Jabberwocky could talk surprised me so much. Maybe it was the fact that he had been playing faithful pet the entire time, or maybe, I was just tired and my brain wasn't working right. Either way, if he could talk that meant he could be reasoned with.

"Of course, I can talk. I am not an animal." He growled through gnashing teeth. His grip on Chess didn't loosen, and it caused me to gasp at the same time that Chess cried out.

"Then why are you working for the bad guy?" I argued, trying and failing to ignore the pressure on my ribs. If he squeezed tight enough to crush Chess' ribs would it break mine? Or would I just feel the pain? I didn't want to find out.

"I owe them a debt and debts must be paid." The fact that he called Dorian a them and not a him proved he knew more about what was going on than I gave him credit for.

"But if you let us go we can get rid of them for you, and your debt won't matter anymore." I winced. The throbbing in my back overrode some of the pain Chess was feeling. I was sure I was probably bleeding, but there was nothing I could do about it now.

The Jabberwocky seemed to think on it for a moment, his other clawed hand coming up to stroke his chin. If I wasn't in so much pain, the sight alone would have made me laugh.

"Debts cannot be forgotten so easily. I am not to hurt you, but they have asked that I persuade you, and that is what I plan to do, starting with your mate here." His claw clamped down around Chess' form and I cried out. His claw had pierced into Chess' side. Blood poured out of the wound and onto the ground below. It took everything I had not to fall to the ground in agony.

The creature glanced between Chess and my gasping form. It seemed to figure something out. He gave Chess another small squeeze that forced me to whimper and drop to my knees.

"How is it that you feel this one's pain?" The curiosity on his face reminded me of a child that had just figured out how to pull the head off its doll.

"It's a long story," I said between gasps of pain. "Bandersnatch. Exchange of magic. Now we're connected." I gave a short laugh that turned to a groan. "I guess it wasn't a long story after all."

"I see." The Jabberwocky mused, humming in its throat. "Will you die if I kill this one?" he gave Chess a little shake that made both of us cry out.

"I...I don't know." I wheezed. "But I wouldn't chance it if I were you." I had to find some way to get him to drop Chess. Any more of this and I wasn't going to be of much use myself.

Pushing the pain away while the creature thought about it, I gathered up my magic until it hummed along my skin. Chess made a startled noise, and I shook my head at him. *Don't draw attention to me* I thought hard at him.

The dragon was still thinking when I shoved the power into the ground. The ground rippled and sprouted little plants. The dirt rumbled beneath our feet and the creature's attention turned back to me but it was too late.

Thick vines shot out of the ground toward the Jabberwocky. They wrapped around his throat, around his arms and legs, jerking him from all sides. He roared and ripped at the vines, dropping Chess in the process.

The moment Chess hit the floor it was like all the air had been knocked out of me, but I didn't stop. I kept shoving magic into the ground, bringing more and more vines to the surface to trap the Jabberwocky.

He tried to shred the vines, but they were too thick, and there were too many of them coming at him at once. I was about to push more magic into it when out of the corner of my eye, I saw where Chess had fallen, right in the path of where the Jabberwocky was being dragged to the ground. In a quick thought, I redirected some of my energy toward where he lay. The vine wrapped around him like a cocoon and delivered him to the ground next to me.

With Chess safe by my side, I turned back to the task at hand. The Jabberwocky was down on its knees. His arms and legs were firmly trapped beneath my pile of vines, and thus, he was reduced to biting at them.

For each vine he chewed through, five more replaced them. I knew I couldn't keep it up much longer. I already felt that edge that usually sent me into a power hungry frenzy. I wasn't sure I was strong enough to come back from it this time. When I was about to give up and make a run for the tear, Chess' hand landed on top of mine, and a rush of magic shot through me and into the earth.

New vines shot from the ground and encircled the Jabberwocky's jaw, closing its mouth from doing any more damage. He struggled for a moment, and I worried he might break out, but then he stopped moving, his dark red eyes gleaming at us in a silent rage.

I knelt there on the ground just breathing. I'd stopped him. I beat a fucking dragon! I gave a short laugh at the realization. When I turned to Chess to brag my smile fell.

Chess lay beaten and bloodied on the ground. His eyes were closed and his chest barely moved up and down. I reached a hand out to him, trying to find the wound on his side to stop the bleeding.

The cut was not as bad as the ones he had suffered by my mother's hands but still bleeding enough to cause worry. Grabbing the edge of Chess' shirt, I yanked it until it ripped. Balling the shirt up, I pressed it against the wound. It caused a groan from Chess and a sharp pain in me that left me gasping.

"Kat." My name fell from his lips, and his eyes fluttered open, the orbs glazed over from the pain.

I shushed him and lifted one hand to stroke his face. "Save your strength."

The stubborn cat ignored me and tried to reach out to me. "You have to go on. Finish this. I'll be all right." He groaned and stopped to catch his breath before giving me a weak smile. "I've healed worse than this, kitten."

"But I can't just leave you, what if the Jabberwocky gets loose?" my gaze swept over the bound creature still glaring at us.

"He did his part. Once you are gone, I don't think he will bother me anymore." His words came out strained and slow. While he told me he was fine, I could feel that he wasn't. If he was feeling even half of what I was, he couldn't be. But did I really have a choice?

I grabbed his hand, placing it on the spot where mine had been pressing against the wound. I placed a hand on either side of his face and leaned in close.

"Don't you die on me, Cheshire." I pressed my forehead to his, closing my eyes briefly. "When I get back we are going to get you stitched up and I'll play nurse to you for as long as you want." I gave a small laugh and smiled. "I'll even get a short little outfit to wait on you in."

Chess chuckled at this and then winced. "Sounds lovely, pet."

I pressed my mouth to his, careful of his side as I leaned into him. His lips met mine in a lingering kiss that didn't last long enough before whispering, "I love you."

"And I you." His emerald orbs gazed at me softly before he gestured with his head. "Go, end this."

Pulling back, I nodded; my eyes burning from unshed tears. Whether it would end with my death or not, it would be over soon.

I stood from the ground and gave one prolonged look back over my shoulder at Chess. I gave him a thumbs up and a smile before turning back to the hole. I rounded my shoulders and stepped through the tear. It was time to kick some Shadow ass.

THE BETWEEN. THE God damn fucking Between. If there was one place in the universe I wished never to be again it was here.

The world was white and seemed never ending, like the inside of a bleached butthole. There was nothing there but the tear and a dark shadow in the distance. I could still feel Chess' pain, and I steeled myself against it as I forced my feet to move toward the shadow.

As I approached it, a sickening, evil feeling overwhelmed me. The shadow wasn't Dorian. It couldn't be. It was too vile, to full of darkness to be my ex-fiancé.

It was, though. Or part of it was. The person—the creature standing before me was not a full person anymore. Cloaked in a cloud of black darkness that seemed to leak from every pore, the Shadow man stood waiting, his back to me. When my footsteps reached him, he turned slowly, his hands out to the side as if to welcome me into his embrace.

"Katherine," his voice burned my ears, and I felt a jolt in my stomach at the sound of my full name. "How nice of you to join us. I can rest assured that my pet did his work well, or did our lovely Moderator skip out?"

"Never," I spat, angry that he would even suggest such a thing. "I am here to end this. Once and for all."

"End this?" his eyebrows raised, a mock innocent look on his face. "But it has only just begun. Join us and we can show you so much more than you could have ever dre—"

"No," I snapped cutting him off. "No more talking. This ends now." I forced a full glamour onto my hand, causing my nails to grow and sharpen. "Blood of like blood, my heart to yours, return to the realm from which you came and dwell here no longer." My voice resounded through the air, my hand poised and ready to swipe the sharpened claw along my palm.

The creature that had been Dorian's eyes filled with panic at my words, but then they fell to my hands where I was about to cut my palm open and smiled. "Very well. We accept."

I frowned, confusion etching my face. "You accept? You can't accept I haven't cut my hand yet. The blood hasn't been paid."

They laughed, the sound of it echoing out into the Between. "Oh, but you have. Blood has been spilled and we accept."

Horror filled me, and in what seemed like slow motion, my eyes fell to my hands where they were still drenched in Chess' blood. My eyes flew back up to the creature that Dorian had become, their laughter grew as they began to glow and ripple.

I spun on my heel and shot for the tear that led back to the Willow. My feet didn't seem to move fast enough, and I wished for once that I could transform into an owl like Dorian. To move faster, to be stronger.

Before my feet even hit the dirt I knew I was too late. The hole was back and only getting bigger, but still I searched out where I had left Chess. My eyes took in the now empty blood covered spot on the ground and I couldn't breathe.

Chess was gone.

CHAPTER 20
THE AFTERMATH

I SPENT THE first month after the ordeal in a stupor, refusing to see anyone and only leaving my room long enough to find another bottle of alcohol to try to numb myself. But it never worked. Nothing did.

Mab's warning to me before I had given my magic to Chess had not been severe enough. If I had known it would be this painful, this gut wrenching emptiness that made each day seem like torture, I probably still would have gone through with it. I just would have given Chess more shit about it. I definitely wouldn't have let him out of my sight.

After the first month, Alice had come into my room, wrinkled her nose in disgust, and demanded I get out of bed. I promptly threw her out with a little magic and created a barrier of vines over the entrance. I quickly realized I hadn't thought that one through when I had to remove the vines not more than ten minutes later to relieve my bladder.

That's when she pounced.

"Shit!" I cried out, still sitting on top of the toilet. I leaned forward, grabbing the towel off the rack to cover up and glared at her. "What the fuck, ever heard of privacy?"

Alice stuck her nose in the air and looked down on me with as much haughtiness as a queen. "Not when you are hurting yourself and those around you."

"How am I hurting anyone?" I questioned, flushing the toilet and wiggling my pants up my legs while trying to stay covered with the towel. "I've been in my room this whole time. No way to hurt anyone in there. Not anymore." My throat clogged up at my words, and I forced the guilt back. I needed more alcohol.

"You also aren't helping anyone." Alice stepped in front of the bathroom door, her arms crossed over her dress shirt, tapping her partly covered heel on the tile floor.

"So? I did my job there's nothing left to do." I shrugged, turning instead to wash my hands. I chanced a glance in the mirror and winced. My face was pale and I had bags under my eyes. My hair looked like a rat had started a nest in it from not seeing a brush in over a month. Not that it mattered. Nothing mattered anymore.

Alice huffed at my answer, irritation pinching her face. "You think just because the Shadows are gone people don't need you? What about Mop and Trip? They've come by every day asking for you, and I have to turn them away, because you are acting like a selfish child."

Anger prickled in me at her words. "Selfish? So choosing to give my life to save everyone else, and then to have the love of my life taken from me, is selfish? Asking for just a little time to mourn? You surely need to rethink the definition of the word."

Her face fell at my words and pity filled her eyes. "But you haven't mourned. You've done nothing but numb yourself with drink. You barely eat. From the circles under your eyes, I doubt you get any sleep." She placed a hand on my arm and gave it a squeeze. "I know you miss him. We miss him too, and I can't imagine what you are going through—"

"That's right you can't. So stop trying to." I jerked my arm away from her and pushed my way into the hallway.

Hurried footsteps followed me, and Alice's voice continued, "But there are things that have to be finished. Holes that need patching up." Her words came out quickly as she chased me into the kitchen. "The first step to healing yourself is to start by healing others."

"Where'd you hear that an AA brochure." I snorted, opening the fridge and frowned at the lack of alcohol inside.

"You won't find any of that vile drink. I threw it all out."

I glared at her and slammed the door to the fridge shut. "Fine. I'll go buy some more."

"Can't." she gave me a smug grin before I could even reach for my keys.

"And why not?" my hands balled up into fists, the anger I had before flaring up into rage. Magic prickled along my skin, and I almost smirked when Alice gave a wary step back before she straightened her spine and stared me down.

"I called your mother and had her take it. I told her I didn't trust you to not hurt yourself in the state you are in right now.

So she took it away." She fluttered a hand in the air.

"Since when are you and my mom such pals?" I snarled, not really believing she would call my mother on me.

A small smile crept up her face and a gleam filled her eyes. "Oh, you would be surprised what kind of friends you can make when you have something in common."

"And what would that be? Manicures? Charity?" I scoffed and turned toward the back door. It was dark outside; a quick glance at the clock showed it was after seven. What day of the week was it? I didn't even know what month it was anymore.

"You," Alice said simply, moving up beside me.

"Why do you even care?" I sighed, my anger slipping out of me easily. I was just so tired.

"Because there is still disarray in the Underground and a whole slew of Fae who do not want to go back. Because there is a tear in the middle of the UnSeelie Court that we can't fix. And maybe, because you are my friend." Slipping an arm around my waist, Alice drew me out the back door and into the garden.

Moonlight shone down in the back yard covering everything with a gray film. The air smelled different, clearer. But I guess being stuck in a room with the same stagnant air for over a month would make anything smell better.

I let Alice lead me through the garden and through the trees. I didn't know where we were going. I didn't ask and Alice didn't offer. We just kept walking until we began to walk through a familiar clearing and the babble of water reached my ears.

My eyes landed on the pond and hidden alcove that had brought me to the Underground in the first place, I stopped. "Why did you bring me here?"

She gestured in front of her with a small sad smile. "To mourn."

I followed the direction her arm was pointing. There was a new addition to the surrounding foliage. A willow tree that I knew for certain hadn't been there before stood tall and proud a little ways away from the pond. I stepped toward it and then my feet moved on their own until I was running.

My heart racing in my chest, I shoved the hanging vines aside and made my way to the base of the tree. I fell to my knees before a throne, identical to the one that had been at the base of Chess' willow, vibrant purple vines and all. At the foot of the throne were bouquets of flowers, someone's teddy bear, candles, and other items.

I had worried that after the Shadows were gone nobody but me would care that Chess was gone. That they would think good riddance and move on with their lives. Seeing these things in honor of him brought tears to my eyes. Once the tears started, I couldn't stop them.

I wailed and beat the ground. I cursed God for taking him from me. Most of all I cursed myself for letting it happen.

The entire time I cried, Alice stood by my side. Not speaking. Not offering a hug or a hand. Just waiting. Like she knew I wouldn't accept it even if she offered. Which I wouldn't have. I pretended it was because I was too strong for that, but it was really because the moment anyone gave me comfort, I clung to it and had a hard time bringing myself back together.

After a while, my sobs finally ebbed, and she knelt beside me. "We didn't have a ceremony, well, because it would be silly when there was no body to bury, but we just let people come as they wanted to. No judgment, no pressure." She gave a small laugh. "You'd be surprised by how many showed up that first day and how often some come by just to tell him about their day. Mop particularly."

"Mop?" I jerked my head up at the sound of the brownie's name. "How is he?"

"Oh, he is getting by like we all are, but they miss you." A forlorn expression covered her face. "We all do."

"I know." I ducked my head in shame. "It's hard, you know? Without him. Not just because he is gone, even though it is partly that, but when he left, it felt like a part of me left with him. A piece that is still out there somewhere. It tugs at my heart and keeps me up at night."

"Mab said this would happen. Maybe she knows a way to make it not as bad?" she turned her head to the side in thought.

"Maybe," I murmured.

I stared up at the throne. My mind meshing my memory and the scene before me, making it seem like Chess was still sitting there on his throne with one leg thrown over the side and a crop stick playing between his fingers as he smiled boyishly. My heart clenched at the sight, and I shook my head to be rid of the image.

"Should we head back?" Alice started to stand from the ground, but I placed a hand on her arm.

"Would it be okay if we just sat here for a while?" I wasn't ready to go back yet. Alice had been right when she said I needed to mourn, but more than anything, I needed to be outside. What better place than to do both of those things than at the feet of a hero? Because that is what Chess was. Not a waste of space. Not an unwanted. Not even a half-breed. He was a hero, even if he wasn't just mine.

Alice grinned at me and knelt back down. "Of course, as long as you need."

It turned out I needed more time than I thought. I ended up falling asleep at the base of the tree. When I awoke, there was a blanket thrown over me and a few of the candles had been lit. In the dim morning light, I saw there was a note next to me from Alice.

Was called back to the house. Take as much time as you need, I'll come check on you in the morning.
— A

Standing from the ground, I picked the blanket up into my arms. I walked up to the throne and rubbed my hand along the arm of the chair. I took one last look at the shrine the citizens of the Underground had built for him, and for the first time in over a month, I walked back to the house with a smile on my face and a song in my heart. And this one was for Chess.

EPILOGUE

CHESHIRE

MY HANDS POUNDED on the glass as I watched Kat run a hand over her face. She was pale and had dark purple circles under her eyes. Her hair was a mess, but to me, she had never looked more beautiful. Now if only I could get her to hear me.

"I do not know why you bother, she can't hear you." A smooth and husky voice slithered down my spine that was followed by a pale hand tipped with black nails that clapped me on the shoulder. I fought not to shrug it off, knowing it would only encourage her further.

"I have to try," I growled, stepping away from one of the many mirrors surrounding me.

The Shadow Realm was not like I had pictured it. While it was dark, it was more of a permanent night than complete darkness. There was even a ball of light that hung from the sky. I was thankful for that light a little more every day. With Morgana here, there was no telling what would happen if I was left in the dark with no way to see her advances.

"You can try all you like, it won't make a difference. Though, I think it's cute how dedicated you are to reaching your love." Morgana's pouty red lip opened up wide as she laughed, and I tried not to shiver at the sound.

I moved away from where she stood, her long, blood red gown enveloped her like a one size too small glove, causing her chest to be dangerously close to spilling out. At one time I would have gladly accepted her advances, would even have encouraged it, but after meeting Katherine, everything changed.

She didn't see me as a half-breed or even as the Moderator. She didn't damn me or fear me for my powers, she accepted me. Even before she knew she was the princess.

Being apart from her was more torture than the Shadow Realm could ever be.

When I had first arrived, it was Morgana who had found me passed out and leaning against a dead log. She had taken me to her home and taken care of my wound until I was well enough to get around on my own. If I had known that taking her help would mean that I owed her my affection in return, I would have rather rotted out there with the log. Instead, I was forced to have her as my constant shadow as I maneuvered the nightmare realm.

At first, I had wondered why it was called that when there wasn't anything nightmarish about it at all. Perpetual night? All right, not a problem. No plant life or trickling streams. That would have been a problem had I not been Fae. I wouldn't starve for a very long time. I planned to be out of here before that happened. Last but not least, was the annoying woman who would not take no for an answer. While that was unpleasant it wasn't exactly nightmarish.

What was a nightmare were the mirrors. They were everywhere. Every step I took I ran into a mirror that showed me people and places I knew. I could see them, hear them, but they couldn't see me. I'd been trying for weeks to get through to someone, anyone, but they never responded. Never even acted like they noticed anything different.

I had thought Kat would be different. We were connected. She would surely hear me. But since I got here, where I would have normally felt her was just a gaping hole of nothingness. Each day that passed with no response, it seemed to grow bigger and bigger. Maybe one day it would get big enough to swallow me up. Then at least I would be put out of my misery.

Shaking my head at the depressing thought, I moved to the mirror that overlooked her room and waited. I was going to get through to her. If it took days, weeks, or even years. I would get out of here if my name wasn't Cheshire S. Cat!

Thank You for Reading!

Want to find out what happens to Kat next?
Find out in Chasing Shadows.

Don't stop there! Find out how it all started with these two prequels.
Lynne & Dorian's story: Chasing Hearts
Alice's story: The Crimes of Alice

About the Author

Erin Bedford is an otaku, recovering coffee addict, and Legend of Zelda fanatic. Her brain is so full of stories that need to be told that she must get them out or explode into a million screaming chibis. Obsessed with fairy tales and bad boys, she hasn't found a story she can't twist to match her deviant mind full of innuendos, snarky humor, and dream guys.

On the outside, she's a work from home mom and bookbinger. One the inside, she's a thirteen-year-old boy screaming to get out and tell you the pervy joke they found online. As an ex-computer programmer, she dreams of one day combining her love for writing and college credits to make the ultimate video game!

Until then, when she's not writing, Erin is devouring as many books as possible on her quest to have the biggest book gut of all time. She's written over thirty books, ranging from paranormal romance, urban fantasy, and even scifi romance.

Also, third person is really weird when writing about yourself. Just putting that out there.
Come chat me up!
www.erinbedford.com
Facebook.com/erinrbedford
twitter.com/erin_bedford
Don't forget to follow me on Goodreads, Pinterest, Instagram, and YouTube!

Want to be the first to know about my new releases?
Erinbedford.com/newsletter

Made in the USA
Monee, IL
15 July 2022